River
Song

River Song

by BELINDA HOLLYER

Holiday House / New York

If you haven't heard Maori words spoken, you won't know that the "wh" sound is like an English "f." So "taniwha" is "tan-i-fah," with more or less equal stress on all syllables.

Text copyright © Belinda Hollyer 2007
First published in 2007 by Orchard Books
338 Euston Road, London NW1 3BH
United Kingdom
First published in the United States of America by Holiday House in 2008
All Rights Reserved
Printed in the United States of America
www.holidayhouse.com
First American Edition
1   3   5   7   9   10   8   6   4   2

Library of Congress Cataloging-in-Publication Data

Hollyer, Belinda.
River song / by Belinda Hollyer.—1st American ed.
p. cm.
Summary: Jessye loves living with her grandmother in a traditional
Maori village, but when her freewheeling mother comes back into
her life, Jessye must decide whether to stay or move to the city.
ISBN-13: 978-0-8234-2149-7 (hardcover)
[1. Mothers and daughters—Fiction.   2. Grandmothers—Fiction.   3. Maori
(New Zealand people)—Fiction.   4. New Zealand—Fiction.]   I. Title.
PZ7.H7313Riv 2008
[Fic]—dc22
2007035995

My grateful thanks to Elspeth Sandys and
Kylie Ngaropo, who both read the final draft of this book
and made many excellent suggestions.

Kylie also lent Jessye her own mihimihi—nga mihi mahana
ki a koe e Kylie mo tou tautoko mai.

Chapter One

I have discovered that you can go along for ages without seeing things as they really are. And then one day their true colors light up as clear as the sun in the morning. They come in so close you can't ignore them: They tap you on the shoulder or grab you by the arm, and won't let go until you listen to what they have to say. And what I remember best about the day my destiny gave me the nod, was sprawling on the sofa in the river house beside Nana, listening to her sing.

We'd been standing side by side just before that, singing a traditional Maori song, which I was learning with my eyes closed. That might sound weird, but in the old days you'd have learned songs at night, in the dark. Practicing with your eyes closed is the closest you can get to that in the daytime, and Nana's keen on teaching me the old ways when she can. And I enjoy the strangeness of building up the words and the tune, line by line, and hearing Nana next to me, although I can't see her—it's a bit like a dream. A good one. But our practice was over and now Nana was singing a different kind of song—the sort you can sit down for.

Nana's singing is one of the great things about her. The richness and power of her voice filled my head; I could feel it vibrate in my ears and buzz down the back of my throat. She knows songs I've never heard anywhere else. Maori waiata, of course—even the ancient chants that hardly anyone remembers. And she can sing hymns and pop songs and country music, but what she likes best are what she calls piano songs. When Nana was a bit older than me, she lived up in town with some cousins so she could go to high school; there weren't good country schools back then. Her cousin's mother's sister had a piano, and everyone gathered there on Friday nights, Nana said, to sing around the piano.

"I learned songs," she told me, "just from hearing them sung. We sang anything and everything, as long as someone could play it. Words are easy to remember if you have a tune to carry them."

The song she sang in the river house that day was the old Irish one about a minstrel boy. I know the words by heart—like Nana says, it's easy if you have the tune in your mind. It starts like this:

> *The minstrel boy to the war is gone,*
> *In the ranks of death you'll find him;*
> *His father's sword he has girded on,*
> *And his wild harp slung behind him.*

It's a song that scoops you up and carries you along with it. Not only the words, but the way the tune swells up and comes to collect you. And then it lifts you high for the last bit, and brings you home again.

When the song finished, we sat quiet for a few moments, enjoying what I call the not-song time that follows a song. At first the silence in the room—the not-song—echoed in my ears, and it was all that I could hear. But when that sank away, I knew other sounds would take up their place again: the ticking of the clock on the shelf above the stove; the cicadas outside in the garden; the far clear call of birds in the forest across the river. Nothing much else, though, right now; it was a quiet afternoon in Waimotu.

I felt Nana, beside me, shift back on the sofa to glance out through the side window. I knew why; Nana was looking to see if she could see Mum's car on the road. But I didn't think Mum would be coming yet. She was more likely to catch a later ferry than the one that would've just docked, and there's only one ferry across the harbor every hour. Nana was looking out, anyway.

I leaned forward so I could see past Nana and through the screen door. The river water was well on the turn now, with the tide pulling down from the mouth of the harbor. I could see where the current stretched the water into tight lines of ripples, silver and gray and pale green all at once. The edges of the river under the mangroves were still covered: more water than mud there. It looked water-shifty and liquid with light, rather than mud-dull and solid like pencil lead, but that would change with the tide.

There was nothing on the river road; no cars or trucks, and no one walking, either. I thought Mum would probably drive, but her cars came and went according to the people she'd borrowed them from wanting them back, and whether or not they'd start on any given morning. So she could've caught the bus down, or got a ride to the harbor and come over on the ferry as a foot passenger. Nana was probably looking out for a person on the river road. A walker would take longer to get here than a car.

"Okay, girl, time to get on," said Nana, and she pulled herself up with a bit of a grunt. Not the best moment to remind her what she always said, that people shouldn't make noises getting up and sitting down, no matter how much their bones ached. "It's an old person's trick, eh? That 'ouff' sound," Nana would say with a glint in her eyes. "Don't want to start on those before my time." It was a joke between us that she was really only as old as me. Other times she claimed to have lived as long as a taniwha, a water monster, from the time of the old stories. It depended on her mood and how tired she was.

Right now she was getting ready to make a lemon cake. That's Mum's all-time favorite; she always says so, especially when Nana makes it. I like banana cake best overall, but I do love the sugary lemon sauce that gets poured over a warm lemon cake as soon as it's out of the oven. The sauce soaks in and makes the cake sort of sweet and sour at the same time. Awesome.

"This'll go down well, eh?" she said. I nodded slowly;

it wasn't that I didn't agree right off, but Nana likes it when I'm thoughtful. "Jessye girl," she says, "you're always rushing, tutu-ing around like I don't know what. Slow down! Let's have a pause for breath and a moment to think!" And I wanted to please her, because she was making the cake to please Mum.

While Nana started mixing the dry ingredients, I went out the back to choose lemons from the tree. It could be two small lemons or one large one for a lemon cake; one large one was a better choice because big lemons are juicier and it's easier to grate the rind. Then you need another lemon for the sauce, and a small one's fine for that as long as it's juicy.

I stopped on the doorstep, catching a sudden blur of movement across the backyard. A kingfisher? The right size for one but too fast to be certain. I gently stirred the cat sleeping against the drain cover with my toe, but he just stretched and then elaborately re-curled himself without even bothering to look up. Nana always had cats, sometimes two or three at once, but right now there was only Tu, Nana's old rusty brown cat who never wanted to play or socialize with humans, not even with Nana, who said he'd been the liveliest kitten she'd ever known. Maybe Tu had used up all his playfulness, with none left for his old age. I longed for a cat of my own, or a dog. But when you don't live in one place all the time it's hard to have a pet. I tried to talk Nana into it once, but she quickly pointed out the difficulties.

"Tu would hate another cat, and he wouldn't tolerate a

dog of any size, you know how he is with Joe's old sheep-dog," she'd said. And I did know. Tu might look peaceful and spend most of his time sleeping, but when a dog comes onto the property, even one on a leash, even one he knows, he goes crazy. He launches himself from nowhere like a missile and attaches himself to the dog's back in a blur of claws and yowls and spitting. Joe's sheepdog takes off every time, yelping with shock and the sheer indignity of it all, with Tu hanging on to his back like a circus rider until he judges it time to jump down and strut proudly away from the chaos he's created. Nana named Tu after the Maori god of war. She got that right.

"And even if we got you a kitten, say, and even if Tu put up with it, no guarantees on that, then when you go away what would the kitten do?" Nana had continued. "I couldn't keep it for you because of Tu and you couldn't take it along, not necessarily. Cats like being settled in one place, they can't be dragged around to fit your fancy." She gave me a quick hug. "Do what you can with what you have, girl," she said. "Don't spend your life wanting what you don't have."

When I took the lemons back inside, my face must have still had a wishing-for-what-I-didn't-have shape. Nana glanced at me and smiled; she can always read my moods straight off.

"Make lemonade, eh, Jessye?" she said. "That's what they say. If they give you lemons, make lemonade."

I thought about that.

"Like, make the best of things," she went on. "Turn

things to your advantage. Take a sour old thing and make it fresh and lively, like sweet lemonade."

"Could we make lemonade?" I asked. "I mean the real fizzy stuff, not the way you mean about making the best of things?"

Nana went on grating lemon rind into the bowl. Then she nodded.

"If I can think how it's done. You know, it was my nana used to make it in the old days. Then I made it for my own boys every summer, mine and everyone else's young ones, it seemed like. You need something extra—citric acid maybe—but I don't remember how much to how many. I'll check my books, eh; might even have some of that acid put away."

It was unusual for Nana to mention her boys, and I wish I'd taken her up on it. But I stuck with what was in my mind, instead.

"Does Mum like lemonade, d'you reckon?"

Nana glanced at me again as she stirred in the rind and the juice. "Not that I know of. Ask her, eh?"

"When she comes." I felt brave saying "when." We both knew that Mum might come on the next ferry or the one after that, or she might not come at all. There had been lots of times that Mum hadn't arrived when she was expected, when she'd said she'd come. Not even the day after, come to think of it. But despite all that, I still thought she would come today.

"When she comes," agreed Nana calmly, concentrating on pouring the cake mixture into the buttered pan. I opened the oven door for her and the cake went in safely.

"Forty minutes, give or take," said Nana.

"I'll clear up and watch it for you," I offered. I knew Nana might want to have a rest while we waited for at least one more ferry and Mum's arrival.

When Nana had gone into the bedroom and pulled the patchwork quilt up over her legs against the possibility of flies, and after I brought her a glass of water in case she got thirsty, and promised a cup of tea when the cake was done, the house settled back into stillness. Nana isn't quick in her movements, but there is always a sort of swirl of air around her, and the space she leaves behind seems to wait for her to come into it again.

If I'm worried about anything, as long as I know where Nana is I'm fine. My earliest memory is Nana bending over me in the night and tucking a blanket around me, with her braid of dark hair falling forward across her shoulder and tickling my nose. I'd probably had a bad dream and she'd come to soothe me. But because of the tickle and just having her there, I can't remember the bad dream at all, only the comfort.

She isn't a pushover, my nana. She has firm ideas about what's right and what isn't, and she lets me know if I step over any of her lines. But she's always there. I don't mean she's always standing next to me, I just mean when she is with me she doesn't go off somewhere else in her head and forget about me.

She's like my bottom line—which is what Uncle Joe would say. He does bookkeeping, and the bottom line's the last line of the arithmetic, after you've added all the money you've earned and subtracted everything you've spent. And that's what matters in keeping accounts, Joe says, because it's what everything comes down to in the end: what you've got left.

But I'd rather think of Nana as my known world, like an explorer would say. I don't know any explorers but I've read about them, how hundreds of years ago they sailed out across the oceans, some of them even fearing that the world was flat and they'd fall right off the edge, but knowing that they wanted to discover something, make a new life happen. Doing it all by the stars or by instinct in big double-hulled canoes, or in sailing ships that weren't much bigger than canoes.

I couldn't do any of that, I don't think it's any part of my destiny. I love to hear about such adventures, but I'd be frightened to sail into unknown seas. Maybe if Nana came along I'd be okay, but she doesn't like the sea so she probably wouldn't come. She says wild water's dangerous, that it can't be trusted.

I washed up the cake-making things first. I had to keep an eye and a nose on the cake, but apart from that, about thirty minutes lay in front of me and every one of them was mine.

I decided to write in the book Joe gave me. It's a hard-covered exercise book with lines down the pages for keeping accounts, like how much money comes in and goes out: all that bottom-line stuff. I use it to write down the words of songs and do pictures to go with them. Nana's songs, mostly, and some from Joe, too. He knows just about every country song ever written—lots from America and Australian bush ones and old New Zealand songs as well. This is quite surprising if you only know him for profit-and-loss arithmetic. Joe tends to go for the things in life that you can see and touch, but then he sings about lost love and loneliness like he could reach out and touch them, too. He says there's all the wisdom of the world in his songs, not that I can see that, but he could be right. What I have noticed is that his songs tell sad stories, but they have cheerful tunes. If you couldn't hear the words, you'd think it was happy hour.

I write down other stuff, too, like a list of names for the kitten or puppy I might have one day. I can add the recipe for lemonade when Nana remembers it, but in the meantime I wanted to put down her lemon-cake recipe. Then if I went back to town with Mum, and if Mum wanted lemon cake while I'm there, I could make it for her. It's not hard to do, but I mightn't remember measurements on the spot unless I wrote them down, so I got out Nana's recipe book. I already knew about buttering the pan and being generous in the corners where the cake might stick, and about how long it took in the oven, so I only wrote what I might forget—like how much flour and sugar and butter and how many eggs. Then I drew a picture of a lemon tree with two lemons—one big and one little, for the cake and the sauce. I added Tu asleep under the tree because I like drawing him, even though he's not an ingredient, and he won't even be around if I make the cake by myself.

I kept glancing at the clock so as not to forget about the cake that was baking right now, and after twenty minutes I opened the oven door just a crack and peered inside to see what was happening. Sometimes Nana turns things around in the oven or moves them up or down a shelf at the halfway point, but I didn't do that because the cake looked as though it was coming along just fine.

I was still enjoying the peacefulness when I realized I'd been hearing a distant truck on the road for several minutes without really noticing it. It had begun as a low, far-off machine noise, but once I started to think about it, I could hear the truck engine shifting down through its gears, so it could start pulling up and around the long, slow bend in the road. Probably a timber truck going up to the mill.

But if it was going to the mill, why would the engine be slowing again as it got closer? The trucks never slow down for the steep bends on our road unless they can't help it— unless they're going to stop.

This one was really slowing down, and then it stopped completely with a hiss of hydraulic brakes and a shaking cascade of engine revs. Just down the road by the sound of it.

I went to the front door. You can see the road from there, but not the bit where the truck was because the fringe of mangroves blocks the view. But I heard a man shout and a woman laugh and the slam of the cab door, and then the truck started off again and passed the gate on to Nana's property. It was a timber truck, and I glimpsed the driver's red shirt. There was no one still in the cab with him.

Then everything happened at once. Mum walked

around the bend of the road swinging her backpack and opened the gate. Nana came out of the bedroom, Tu meowed at the window, the cake started to smell good, and the clock struck five.

It's only when I look back on that day that I can see how it was a moment of destiny for me, the first hint of what was on its way. I'd never have guessed that my destiny would be foreshadowed by a timber truck.

Chapter Two

Living with Nana—well, it's great. And it's where I mostly am, so in one way it's ordinary. But in another way it's almost like a holiday where you don't do anything exactly dazzling, but you have a good time in other ways. Kind of a holiday from holidays, like sitting down to chicken soup and whole-wheat toast after weeks of cream cakes and fizzy drinks.

Even going to school when I'm at Nana's is almost a restful experience, although I know that might sound weird. But the school here in Waimotu is small so I always know everyone's name from day one, and I fit back in with no hassle when I've been away. And I like the way the classes are mixed up together, so we have the little kids in one corner of our room and help them with reading or spelling.

When I'm living at the river house, coming back after school is always good, too. I can smell dinner cooking mixed with the background smell of the house, and I just close my eyes and sniff it all up. There's the soap Nana scrubs everything with, even herself, and that smells good to start with. There's lavender from the polish she uses, and from the flowers she dries and hangs in big bunches by the stove. There's often the edge of an earthy smell, too, from whatever Nana's working on. It might be from potting up seeds for her veggie garden, or from a bag of feathers and seeds and plants she's gathered for one of her weaving projects. Even with my eyes closed I can tell exactly what's what, and where it is in the room.

Living with Mum isn't like that at all. It isn't like a holiday, either, although it might look like one from the outside. Mum's a bit like a romantic gypsy in a story, flitting around without a settled home and not wanting one, either. So being with her is like whirling around on the Ferris wheel at the Easter Show up in town. It's exciting, all sparkling lights and laughing, but after awhile you can't help wishing it would stop.

When the two halves of my life collide, like when Mum comes to Nana's for a day or two, it can be awkward. Nana doesn't like Mum, or maybe it's more that she doesn't approve of her. Nana never bad-mouths Mum if I'm around, and she'd never have a go at her in front of me, but still, I know that's what she thinks. Mum doesn't like Nana much, either, but that's mostly because they're such different people. Someone like Mum'd never be comfortable with someone like Nana; Mum only relaxes with people she thinks won't judge her. Which is why she avoids Joe whenever she's here, because he *really* doesn't like her.

The trouble goes back to when Mum was with my dad. No one's told me exactly why they split up, but I can guess what Nana's opinion would be, whatever happened. I bet she thinks Mum didn't treat him right—Dad, that is, his name's Mikey, and he's Nana's youngest son. Nana always puts her family first, which Dad is and I am, too, ahead of Mum. Mum's family, too, of course, but she's not in the top rank of it as far as Nana's concerned.

Or anyway, Dad was her top-rank family back then, but she won't talk about him now. Dad's the youngest of her three boys, but now there's only Joe around because her middle son died, and Dad's not here. So wouldn't you think she'd want to mention my dad from time to time, even if he's out of favor for some reason? But that's not so. I don't know why not, but she just won't. She tightens her mouth and changes the subject. Once I overheard her talking to Joe when she didn't know I could hear and she said, "Mikey's gone too far; I can't follow him there." That was worse than her saying nothing at all, because her voice was filled with a sort of bitter sadness, so I've stopped asking her; I don't want to make it worse. Joe won't say anything to me, because Nana doesn't want him to. I've tried asking Mum to tell me about him, but she just says, don't ask *me*, I haven't seen him since you were born.

I'd still like to know about my father, though. Even if it was only why I never see him now and why he doesn't ever come to visit, not even to see Nana: She's his mother, for heaven's sake. Nana once said to me that people are like the threads in weaving, they hold one another together. So I don't know why that doesn't apply to my dad.

I do know Mum ran off when I was little and left me

with Nana. And I reckon Mum probably left to get away from my dad, from something he did or something that happened. Sometimes I think she and my dad must have had a big bad fight and never forgave each other. Other times I think they weren't going to stay together, anyway. Mum hasn't been with anyone very long since then; I think she likes moving on.

Being with Mum isn't restful. You never know what will happen next, but there are times when that turns out to be a good thing, and here's an example. For one whole year, when I was six, Mum and I lived in a bus. In its past life the bus had been an ordinary one with rows of seats and a cab for the driver, but by the time we had it someone had taken all that out. They'd put in a wood-burning stove with a chimney cut in the side of the bus, and a big bed up at the front that Mum and I shared. Mum hung a curtain around the bed so I could sleep while she stayed up late at the back with her friends. I used to lie in bed and look through the big curved driver's window at the starry sky and hear Mum talking and laughing down the other end.

I loved that bus. Mum was happy in it and so was I. We never drove anywhere, it was just parked in the garden of one of her friends, and I remember playing with the children who lived in the house. We had a secret spot under a tree where we'd meet and pretend we had mysteries to solve, like in the books Mum was reading to me. Their dad was a potter and he gave us clay to play with and showed us how to make pots from coils of clay. He even fired ours in his kiln alongside his proper, ones.

But after awhile, living in the bus went wrong. There were angry voices shouting and people slamming in and out of the bus, and then a long journey through the night back to Nana's in a borrowed car, with Mum crying all the way.

I still have one of the little clay pots I made, but I don't know what happened to the bus. Maybe someone else lives in it now.

These days, the trouble between Mum and Nana is mostly about me not having a fixed life. Nana doesn't approve, she thinks Mum shouldn't just up and go whenever she wants, and leave me behind. She thinks if Mum's going to leave me with her I should be there all the time. That I should just go to Waimotu school, not jump around whichever schools are near Mum's latest house.

My life isn't just in two halves because I live with Nana sometimes and Mum sometimes. It's also because I was born Maori, and Mum wasn't.

Mum knows Maori stuff, of course, like stories and songs and lots of Maori words for things. And she's part of my Maori family because she married Dad, and because she's my mother. But she hasn't got Maori blood or Maori ancestors, which I do because Dad and Nana are Maori.

Our people are from the Ngapuhi tribe and we can trace our ancestors way, way back hundreds of years to an island in the Pacific Ocean. Well I can't really do that myself yet because I haven't learned the songs and chants about it, but Nana knows them. She says that once you know about your ancestors it's amazing how the world shrinks—she's always finding more people she's related to. When everyone gets together on our marae, which is our local Maori meeting place, I see her having a great time with all the other nanas. They talk away for hours and work out exactly who's who.

I've heard Maori spoken all my life and I understand lots of words, but I can't speak it properly. I'm okay when I'm with Nana on the marae or at school when we do Maori Studies. And I can't do my ancestor chants yet, but I do know how to do my own greeting in Maori. That's a whole lot shorter, because it's only about me. It's how you introduce yourself in the Maori community, and it's called a mihimihi. You name some important things about your Maori identity in a mihimihi—like the canoe that brought your ancestors across the Pacific to New Zealand, the tribe and the family group you're part of, and your river and mountain, as well as your name.

I did mine on the marae for the first time last year; Nana and Joe helped me learn it and made sure I said it right. I was so nervous beforehand I thought I'd pass out, but I felt great after I'd done it. I wrote it down in my book, although I didn't need to because I know it by heart now. Anyway, here it is. In Maori first and then in English, too, because I can do them both.

Ko Ngapuhi te iwi;
Ko Te Rarawa te hapu;
Ko Ngatokimatawhaoroa te waka;
Ko Waimirirangi te tipuna;

Ko Te Reinga te maunga;
Ko Hokianga te awa;
Ko Jessye Marino Cooper ahau.

Ngapuhi is my tribe;
Te Rarawa is my clan inside the tribe;
Ngatokimatawhaoroa is my canoe—the one
my people arrived in;
Waimirirangi is my important ancestor;
Te Reinga is my mountain;
Hokianga is my river;
Jessye Marino Cooper is my name.

Last summer there was a tangi, a funeral, on our marae and people came from all over the country. That's when I met Nellie, although everyone calls her Lovey, who was down from Auckland with her mum and dad. We were all on the marae for the whole thing—24/7 for three whole days—and I met Lovey when we grabbed our pillows at the same time, and put them on the same bench inside the sleeping house. Then we both helped pass around cups of tea to the kaumatua, the old people, which is the time when everyone gets to know one another. So that's when our friendship began. Lovey knew more about who's who than I did, and she pointed out a whole lot of visitors to me I'd never seen before and told me how they fitted in.

Lovey asked me about Nana, who she'd just met. Nana's an important person on our marae, she's a sort of Ngapuhi superwoman and everyone respects her and pays attention to what she says. And when I told Lovey about Nana's house on the river, her eyes widened.

"Is that the river that flooded and someone drowned?" she asked.

I don't know if Lovey's river story is true. We're close friends now so I have discovered she's not a totally reliable person for true stories. She spices them up with bits of her own invention and you can't always tell what's real and what's just Lovey. Her story was about the river flooding in spring and autumn when the tides run high, and our river does that some years, so that's a clue it could be true. Lovey thought it definitely was, because she hadn't heard about anyone else living on the edge of a big river. But it wasn't until she mentioned a taniwha that I started to believe her. I'd heard about the taniwha in Nana's river before.

Some people think taniwha are like dragons or unicorns, that they don't really exist, but some things are real, although you might never see them, and I think taniwha are like that. It's not just me who believes in them, either. Nana says that taniwha stories link us to our history, and they're a way to remember and celebrate our ancestors. Some Maori people can even name taniwha as their ancestors, which gives them a whole heap of prestige, so it's a serious thing. When I asked Nana if she thought taniwha were real she smiled, and asked me in return if I thought the past was real. Well, it is, and it can come into the present, too. Down south, awhile back, a whole new road had to change course because the local people didn't want their taniwha disturbed. As you wouldn't.

Lovey's story was about an angry river taniwha that swept away a riverbank with its lashing tail, and how someone drowned in the flood. She thought that my dad was involved, too, which was a surprise—not that he was the one who drowned, but that he was there when it happened. Lovey said she didn't know any more about it, but I thought she might and just wasn't telling me, because she sort of let the story fall away, which isn't like her at all. Lovey usually goes for dramatic endings to her stories with all the listeners saying "Ooooh!" and looking impressed.

I didn't ask Nana about the story because of Dad being in it, which meant she wouldn't want to say anything to me. And then I forgot about it until much later on.

If Nana and Mum got on better, and if I could settle down in one place with both of them, and if I had a pet of my own, I think my life would be just about perfect. And although I know all that isn't really going to happen, I sometimes think about it, and imagine being in this one place with both of them. My imaginary house is in the country and it looks a bit like Nana's house, but bigger. It has separate bedrooms for all of us, and a big front veranda with a puppy or a kitten and sometimes both of them at once. And a garden with vegetables and flowers all mixed up together, and a field for a pony and a goat.

The pony's mine; the goat is for Nana because she once told me that she liked them so it would be a nice surprise for her. And Mum could get up late and read on the veranda on a swing chair, and paint pictures like she always says she would if she wasn't so busy trying to earn her living, and she could just be herself and be happy.

Even when I'm cross with one or the other of them, I don't want to choose between them. I don't even like to think about it. If I'm honest I wish Mum wouldn't do some of the things that Nana doesn't like, but that's not choosing. I know Mum can't help how she is.

Chapter Three

As soon as Mum arrived on the timber truck that day, things started to go wrong between her and Nana. When Nana heard the truck and saw Mum coming up from the road, she put two and two together and got an answer she didn't like. Mum must have stopped at the pub by the ferry landing for a drink, and that's something Nana hates more than anything. She doesn't drink herself, and she doesn't let anyone drink on her land—and not on Joe's land, either, which is at the back of hers. She gave it to him when he got married, but you'd think she still owned it from the way she sets the rules.

She's completely against alcohol; there's no mistaking how she feels, everyone knows. Including Mum, of course. So when Mum rolled up she had a bright, challenging look in her eye, like she was daring Nana to say something and looking for a fight about it. Nana had on her tight-lipped look that meant she wasn't going to say what she thought. I almost wished she would, though, because the silent disapproval was so loud.

I skipped around getting the cake finished, making tea

in the big teapot, and listening to Mum talk about her journey. I took her backpack off the floor where she'd dropped it, and put it neatly beside the couch like I knew Nana would want, wondering if there was a present for me in it (she doesn't always bring one, but you have to hope), and all the time keeping up a level of chatter to cover Nana's stern looks and Mum's defiance. Trying to keep the peace and move things along.

The mood settled down when we had the lemon cake with a cup of tea. Mum said how good the cake was; even better than she remembered, and Nana relaxed a bit and said that I'd done most of the baking. Mum gave me a big smile and one of her compliments—she has such a sweet voice when she's truly happy and not just pretending. And she said, "Good for you, sweetie," to me in that voice, not in the one she used when she arrived, which had been all spiky with resentment. Her change of mood got to me like it always does, and I could tell that Nana was gratified, too.

So, for a while, it was almost peaceful in the house, like a truce, until Nana sent me out to cut spinach and pick apples and I heard an argument flare up between them. I wasn't listening to the words but I couldn't help hearing their voices, and I couldn't help knowing the fight was most likely about me. I'm the only thing they both care enough about to fight over.

Nana's voice was filled with accusations, and Mum's was sharp edged and crammed with resentment and evasion. Their two voices went back and forth like a two-tone hum of bees, rising and falling, while I cut spinach leaves out in the back garden and looked for three apples more or less the same size for baking. I found a windfall in the long grass under the tree with only a tiny bruise on it and I thought it would do fine, and what's more it was saving food, which would please Nana, maybe even make her less cross with Mum. But when I got near the back door, I heard Mum fling an insult at Nana, the sort that often tipped things too close to the edge and took them somewhere neither of them wanted to go. I suppose you could call Mum brave in that situation; she often chooses to walk straight into danger, even when she doesn't want to deal with the consequences.

"You're as bad as your son! Hard to the core and mean and cruel with it, like Mikey! I don't want that for my child! Jessye needs to be surrounded with love, not hate!"

I stood clutching the spinach and apples, sick with apprehension. Now Nana might lose her temper and tell Mum to go. She did that once before and Mum took her up on it, grabbed her pack and strode off down the road with a much younger me sobbing and running after her. Mum had pushed me away and shouted at me, too; told me to go back and stay with Nana. So I wouldn't be following her this time, unless—

No, it was going to be okay. Mum had started to cry, which meant she was sorry about what she'd said and she'd tell Nana she was sorry, and Nana would be kind in return because she was generous about forgiving and also about admitting the fault of her own quick temper. And then Mum would stay—for dinner and for the night, at least.

But the big question, about whether I would go back to Auckland with her the next day or stay on with Nana, was still up in the air. Sometimes Mum went off without me and I never knew if it was because Nana had put her foot down and said I had to stay, or if Mum had only wanted to check on me and hadn't planned to take me at all.

Visitors always sleep in the front room at Nana's: There's only one bedroom. When I was very little I had a cot by the bedroom window, and then for a while I slept with Nana in her big bed. But later on Nana got a roll-out bed for me, and that's what I still use. Its wheels lock into place when I'm in it, but I can push it away under Nana's bed in the daytime. I like sleeping in the roll-out, it feels snug. If I wake in the night I listen for trains on the line that goes up through the mountains, or for early morning traffic on the river road, and just listening for them and hearing Nana breathing, often sends me back to sleep.

That night, though, I couldn't get to sleep. I listened to Nana and Mum after I went to bed, when they were moving around and getting the couch ready for Mum. They didn't argue anymore; their voices were relaxed and low. Then Nana came to bed and after awhile her slow breathing told me she'd gone to sleep, but it didn't help me do the same. The house was quiet and dark and I was tired, but I was still wakeful. I knew it was late because the ruru owls were silent. A pair of them roost in a pine tree out the back. They hoot at each other to start their night's activities, and then again just before daybreak, when they come back. In the hours between, there's a hoot-free gap when they're too busy hunting to say anything. So I reckon it was after midnight.

Sometimes I count things to help me get to sleep. Nana jokes that it's no good counting sheep because there are so many, you'd never finish. If I'm really wakeful, though, counting anything at all can work against me because I get stuck counting, and that wakes me up even more. So I decided to go outside instead.

I slipped out of bed and glanced at Nana's shape in the big bed. I couldn't see her face because she likes to lie on her right side facing the window and the east. "I like to wake facing the rising sun," she says. I was sure she was asleep, though, and Mum was curled up in a blanket when I tiptoed through the front room. Mum often twists a blanket or a duvet right around her before she lies down, so the wrapping will stay in place all night. "I like the covers tight," is what she says. I know how to turn the front door latch so it doesn't give even a tiny click when you pull it open, so I didn't disturb her when I went outside.

Sitting on the middle step in the moonlight with the house behind me and the dark night around me was so peaceful I felt better immediately. It wasn't cold, and I reckoned I could sit there for ages. I wasn't the only non-sleeper around, either. There were the ruru owls, and Tu liked to hunt at night, too. Lots of wild creatures don't sleep at night.

I wrapped my arms around my knees and stared out over the river. I couldn't see anything clearly, only the suggestion of things, like an artist had roughed out spaces for the trees and riverbank and water, and then gone away to mix up colors or sharpen some pencils. I knew the water was there beyond the mangroves and the trees, though. I could even tell that the tide was out because there were small, sharp, snapping sounds from the mud under the mangroves, oysters maybe, or tiny shrimpy things, sounds that only happen at low tide. Even Nana, who knows tons of stuff about plants and animals, doesn't know what makes the snapping sounds. She says one day we'll put on old clothes and explore the mangroves together, and find out what's making the noise.

I stopped myself from trying to count the snaps.

A bird suddenly cried out from the trees, and then fell silent again. I wondered, do birds have nightmares, or had some other creature disturbed its sleep? I imagined a bird sitting in the mangroves, like I was sitting on the front steps. Something else up late, sitting alone in the dark and looking out at the night.

One of Nana's piano songs goes like this:

> *Sometimes I feel like a motherless child*
> *Sometimes I feel like a motherless child*
> *Sometimes I feel like a motherless child*
> *A long way from home, a long way from home.*

> *Sometimes I feel like a mourning dove*
> *Sometimes I feel like a mourning dove*
> *Sometimes I feel like a mourning dove*
> *A long way from home, a long way from home.*

Sometimes I feel like an eagle in the air
Sometimes I feel like an eagle in the air
Sometimes I feel like an eagle in the air
A long way from home, a long way from home.

I don't exactly know why that appeals to me, it just does. It's a bit sad, which is good for some moods, but I wasn't a motherless child—in fact, you could say I had too many mothers, what with Mum and Nana both trying to bring me up in their different ways. And I wasn't a dove or an eagle, either. I wasn't even a long way from home, because at least when I'm in Waimotu the river house is my home. But I did have an ache that I couldn't get rid of.

Did I want to stay with Nana or go back to town with Mum? Most probably neither of them would ask me what I wanted. Usually they'd tell me what was going to happen once they'd agreed to it between them—or when one of them had given in to the other. So I felt more like a parcel than a mourning dove, to be honest. A parcel that didn't know where it was being sent, that couldn't even read its own address label. It didn't seem fair to have things decided for me. I was absolutely old enough to make up my own mind and to have opinions about my life. I will admit that as long as I wasn't asked, I didn't have to make a choice and hurt whichever one of them I didn't choose. But that didn't mean I liked it.

I had to wonder, what did I want? If I could write the answer down in secret without upsetting anyone, what would I write?

I didn't know. I closed my eyes and imagined a piece of paper and a pen, and then I tried to imagine my handwriting—but no words came. Then I shifted on the step and stared out at the invisible river again. How did everyone else manage, I wondered? Other people I knew had families no closer to perfect than mine. My uncle Joe, his wife, Meri, left him last year and went off down south, and he never sees her now, although she still sends me cards for my birthday and at Christmas.

There are always others at school—at all the schools I've ever been at—who don't have both their parents or live with someone else altogether. I'm not the only one who spends lots of time with their nana, for instance. And I bet I'm not the only one who wishes their mother was a bit different, too. Like I do, with my feelings jangling away in the dark, all muddled up in my heart and my head.

The front door suddenly clicked behind me, and I could tell it was Mum without looking around. She shuffled forward to the steps with the blanket still wrapped around her like a cocoon, and wriggled herself down beside me.

"Can't you sleep, Jayjay?" she asked softly. Jayjay's her pet name for me; no one else ever calls me that. She reached one hand out of the blanket and patted my shoulder.

"I can't, either," she said. "I woke up and I knew you were out here even though I didn't hear you go out, I just *knew* and then I couldn't go back to sleep. Like a part of me was missing—you know?" I could almost hear her smiling at me in the dark. I felt myself being charmed and soothed, every time with Mum it's the same, in the end.

I slid across the step into her waiting hug. I put my head on her shoulder and breathed in the familiar warm, spicy scent from her skin. She always uses the same perfume, although she says her nose is so used to it she can't smell it herself, and she only puts it on for other people to enjoy. I love it, so I'm happy if she puts it on for me.

"I want you to come back with me," she said. "Just for a while. Your nana thinks you should stay in Waimotu because you're doing well at this school. But you can go to school in town, and I miss you, Jayjay, I really do. What d'you say?"

"Does Nana say I can go?" I asked cautiously. I didn't want to be trapped into saying yes, and then discover that Nana hadn't agreed. That had happened the last time and Nana had been upset. But Mum's hand stiffened against me and then she gave me a little slap. Not to hurt, just to show that she disagreed with me.

"It's not for your nana to say yes or no to me," she said. "I'm your mother. I say what's what."

I opened my mouth to answer without knowing what I was going to say, only thinking to stop Mum from going down the road of blaming Nana. I couldn't bear another fight to start up, which was what would happen if Mum started raising her voice and woke Nana up.

But Mum, surprisingly, got in first.

"Monkey in the middle, aren't you, Jayjay?" she said with an awkward little laugh, stroking the shoulder that she'd slapped the moment before. "I know it's not your fault. None of this is your fault, sweetheart. Forget I said that, will you?"

I went back to staring out at the invisible river. Feeling relieved about what she'd just said didn't change the basic situation. I didn't want to leave Nana, I didn't want to disappoint Mum, and I didn't want to have to choose between them.

Head in the sand again, girl? I thought to myself but didn't say out loud.

"Ah, come on, Jessye," said Mum, nudging me. "Don't you want to come back down with me? Just for a while? We can have fun together. We *do* have fun together, don't we?"

"I have fun with Nana, too." I was surprised to hear myself say that. It's the kind of thing Mum doesn't usually like, but she didn't seem to mind.

"Of course you do," she said warmly. "I know that and I'm glad about it. I wouldn't want to leave you here if I didn't think you were happy with her. But you know, Jay-jay, maybe your nana's getting a bit old for all this."

"Too old for *what*?" A tiny stab of fear touched the back of my neck like a cold wind.

"Too old for all this, maybe, is all I mean," she said, waving her spare hand vaguely at both of us on the steps and extending it to include the trees and river as well. "Looking after you, taking care of everything, keeping it all going. . . ."

I twisted around on the step and peered at Mum's face, trying to read her expression in the dark.

"If Nana's getting too old to look after everything, maybe I should stay and look after *her*," I said. "But I don't know where you got that idea. Not from her, I bet. She—she's the same as always, I reckon."

Mum gave me a quick sideways hug. "I know you love her, Jayjay," she said. "But there'll be a day when your nana can't cope anymore, and then what? We'll have to think about that some time. About your future."

I pushed the whole idea out of my head, but the rush of fear brought courage with it.

"Look, Mum," I said, "it'd be fun to go back with you tomorrow. Like you said. But I want to get back here before the end of the term—so some time next month. How about that?" I nudged Mum's knee with my own. The autumn term ended in about seven or eight weeks and it made a kind of natural break that was easy to aim for.

"Well—we'll see, Jayjay," said Mum, patting my knee. "I promise I'll get you back as soon as I can. As soon as it's right. But I want us to have some fun together first. How about *that*?"

I didn't necessarily trust Mum's promises. She isn't always reliable about details like *when* and *how* and *by then*. But I didn't want to fight her and I thought I could make things work out okay, I usually did. Mum likes having me with her, that was true, and I like being with her. And when we have fun together it's more fun than anything else.

Mum once said to me, perfectly seriously, "We owe it to ourselves to have adventures, Jayjay," and boy! did we ever have them! Here's a good example. One time, Mum took me camping. It was just the two of us in an old tent she'd borrowed that turned out not to have enough pegs to keep it up, and even if there'd been enough pegs we didn't know how to keep them in place or stretch the tent tight. It sagged and bagged no matter what we did, and in the middle of the night, in the rain, it suddenly folded up all over us. There we were completely smothered in smelly wet canvas, trying to fight our way out in the pitch dark. I was frightened at first, but Mum was laughing so much she couldn't even push the layers of canvas off us, and then I got the giggles, too, and we both lay there in the rain sobbing with laughter.

"This would be an interesting moment to do our happy dance," Mum had spluttered out when she'd managed to stop laughing, and that set me off again right away. The happy dance thing was something Mum and I had invented one day when we were living on the bus, when I'd been so pleased about something that I started sort of hopping around, first on one leg, then on the other. And Mum laughed and joined in, imitating me, and we developed this routine. The happy dance. We do it together still, sometimes.

Other people have to account to their mothers when they make mistakes or when things go wrong—but it's never like that with *my* mother. When we're together, Mum and I only have each other to account to. She always wants to try out new things, more than I do if I'm honest, and she never minds if they turn out in unexpected ways. But we agreed that neither of us would ever tell another living soul about that tent. It was definitely one of our secrets.

When we stood up to go back inside the house, there was suddenly an enormous splash from the river. Like a sort of slap of a giant fin, flat on the surface of the water. It was very loud and unexpected in the stillness of the night, and it completely got my attention; Mum's, too. We stood still and silent, waiting and listening for a minute or two, but there were no more splashes. Whatever it was had settled back down into the water.

Mum whispered teasingly, "It must have been the taniwha, Jayjay!" And then I remembered out of nowhere what Lovey had told me about the taniwha story and how it involved my family, and just for a moment I wondered if the taniwha was trying to tell me something.

As I finally drifted off to sleep I thought, if Mum makes it hard to get me back to Nana when I want to, I'd just come back by myself.

Chapter Four

I kept an eye on Nana the next morning, but I couldn't spot any signs of her fading like Mum had suggested. Nana always takes awhile to get going in the mornings, so no change there. She says she's like an old car and her battery needs recharging.

And she was okay about me going back with Mum. "But don't you neglect your schoolwork, eh?" she said as we lugged a basket of wet washing out to the line between us. "Make sure you go every day, you'll get behind if you don't, and then it'll be hard to go back, and one thing leads to another. You have to get an education; you're smarter than you know. Can't waste that."

I didn't want to waste my chances, either. That was something Nana and I agreed about, and where Mum was less bothered. I knew Nana had regrets that her sons hadn't been that keen on school; it was only Joe who'd got his qualifications.

"I shouldn't have let them throw away that opportunity, Jessye girl," she'd said to me. "And I won't let you waste it for all the world's riches. You know why not, eh?"

I knew the answer off by heart. "Because a good education is a treasure forever, that's why!" I'd chant back, teasing her. But she's right. I might want to go on to college or art school, so I have to do okay at school now. Mum never got on with school, and she left without taking her exams. She ran off and got a job as soon as she could, she says. Sometimes she goes through the motions of telling me how important school is, but it's just talk, it doesn't come from her heart. She once said that everything important she knows in life she'd learned after she left school. I can see it could be like that, but I don't want to bank on it happening for me, too.

I'm not saying I never want to play hooky, but I know the trouble it causes, so I don't. The last time Mum took me off traveling I missed weeks of the term and the education people found out, and tracked us down. They hauled Mum in for a lecture; Nana even came as well, and I had to do some tests to see if I was up to date with schoolwork. The tests were okay, which was a bit of luck, but without Nana I reckon there would have been even more of a fuss. Nana talked straight with them and explained about me spending time with her. She promised to see things went well with schoolwork whenever I was with her in Waimotu. For her part Mum had promised to send me to school regularly wherever we were, and she kept the promise. Actually I keep it for her—I don't have to be pushed out the door on school days.

It was a fresh, windy morning and the washing dried fast. By the time everything was back inside and folded away ready for ironing, and after Nana had made a big salad for lunch, I could see that Mum was desperate to leave. She'd kept out of the way while we did the wash, sitting on the front steps in the sun painting her toenails. Then she'd come inside and wandered around picking up things and putting them down again, or staring out the windows. Every time there was a car on the road she watched to see who it was, and if it would stop at Nana's. When none of them did, she wandered around the room again, humming under her breath.

"So what ferry are you two aiming for?" asked Nana as I cleared the table. I could have hugged her for sounding so relaxed about it.

"I thought the half past two," said Mum eagerly. "That'll give us time to walk right down to the ferry if we can't catch a ride from someone on the road." She turned to me, smiling. "Got your things ready, Jayjay?"

She had picked the very next ferry so there wasn't much time left before we had to start walking. We couldn't rely on the chance of someone passing in a car to give us a ride. I did have my things ready; I'd organized them while Nana made lunch. I had my notebook and as many clothes as my big backpack would take, plus a warm top because the weather was changing. I didn't need much when I was with Mum because she always kept things like a toothbrush and pajamas for me. She used to hang on to more clothes, but when I started to grow fast they didn't fit me by the time I saw them again.

I went to get my pack and Nana followed me into the bedroom.

"You be good for your mother, eh?" she said gently. I leaned into her hug with my eyes closed, breathing in her scent. Yellow soap, mixed with a warm smell like manuka honey from her skin and hair. I'd know it anywhere, I'm good with smells.

"And go to school every day, eh?"

I nodded my head into the warmth of her body without saying anything. Nana gave me a little shake.

"And phone me if you want to. Phone me, anyway, as often as you like. You know the number, eh?" Nana hardly used her phone except to talk to me when I was with Mum, but it was there on the table by the window, next to a whole range of photos of me. Right from when I was a baby, through to last year in the school play wearing a Victorian costume; we'd done *Waimotu Then & Now* about the timber trade a hundred years ago.

There weren't any photos of Nana's boys, though. I guess she doesn't need a photo of Joe because she sees him most days, but what about the other two? If I ever have children I'll have photos of them everywhere, not just my granddaughter. I wished for a good way to ask her about them again. *I'll find a way when I get back*, I promised myself.

"And come back soon, eh? I'll miss you, you know that?" Nana pushed me away from her slightly so she could see my face. We smiled encouragingly at each other.

"I'll be back before the end of the term," I said. "I told Mum. I'll see you then."

On the ferry, when I opened the side pocket of my pack to get a toffee, I found an envelope folded over and over and tucked inside a plastic bag. Typical Nana, I thought, smiling: she never went in for just one safety pin in case it slipped open, she was a make-sure-the-buttons-are-tightly-sewn-on person. Inside the envelope was a $20 bill, a $10 phone card still in its shrink-wrapping, and a note in Nana's lovely writing on a scrap of paper. FOR EMERGENCIES, the note said. I put the note, the card, and the money in the top pocket of my jacket, which had a secret zipped compartment, and I didn't mention them to Mum.

I stayed outside on the ferry all the way across the harbor. Mum went into the cabin and talked to someone she knew, out of the wind, but I leaned on the rail and watched flocks of gulls wheeling and diving over the fishing boats, while the river flowed fast and strong below me. There were dark streaks and patches of water beside the ferry that swirled and twisted as though they were being tugged by something just under the surface. I remembered the splash in the night, but nothing like that happened in the bright daylight of the river crossing.

Mum's new place was on the far side of Auckland. It took a whole extra bus ride after we'd already done two others, starting from the ferry dock. When we finally turned into Mum's road it was getting dark, but I could guess which house, because Mum's old car was sitting in the road outside.

"Dead battery," she said with a shrug and a grin, and I thought of Nana and her morning joke about herself, but I didn't mention it.

The house was an old wooden one, with cheerful music spilling out the front windows. There were three kids around my age playing cards on the front porch, and my heart lifted when I recognized Amber, who's Robyn's daughter—Robyn is Mum's best friend. Amber's a year younger than me so she's never in my class, but we'd walked to school together from Mum's last house, and I'm always glad to have someone I know in the house, especially at first. Robyn stuck her head out the kitchen window to wave and shout a welcome as we turned up the path. Then she disappeared back inside the house again, and the music stopped, and started up again with a recording that Mum and Robyn both loved—I'd often heard them sing it in the evenings. Robyn's a folksinger and she's good on the guitar, and this is her signature song. She even says she wants it at her funeral! Mum always laughs when she says that, and then she says, "But what about the mountain thyme, eh, lassie? Who's going to bring it?" Because the main part of the words, the bit I remember best, goes like this:

Oh, the summer time is coming
And the trees are sweetly blooming
And the wild mountain thyme

Grows around the blooming heather—
Will you go, lassie, go?

And we'll all go together
To pick wild mountain thyme
All around the blooming heather—
Will you go, lassie, go?

Then Robyn rushed back out and hugged us both, and said, "April! Jessye! *There* you are!" And the "*there* you are!" was another old joke between her and Mum, and Mum laughed and looked all perked up again.

Even with Robyn and Amber around I was cautious, because I can never tell how living with Mum is going to turn out, not right off. I only discover that as the time goes along. I'm good at watching her without her knowing, so I can work out how she's feeling. Sometimes I look at her in a mirror, or through a doorway, to sense her mood. That way she doesn't get a chance just to pretend things are okay, which she tends to sometimes.

I registered at school the next morning. I stood in the corridor outside the princpal's office, waiting to be put in a class, feeling nervous as anything and trying to remember how pleased Nana would be that I was there. But it turned out pretty well, because of two things. One is that my class teacher seemed okay and he likes art, and the other is that— big surprise!—I actually knew someone in my class. It was like a good omen. Monica had been at my last Auckland school, as it happens, but her family had moved while I was back with Nana, and she'd ended up at this one, too. She was more grown up than I remembered; she even had a nose ring, although she wasn't wearing it; there was only the hole. She'd been suspended for a day because she'd forgotten to take the ring out for school. Same old same old is what she said, and I had to agree. Schools have to draw the line somewhere, I can see that's fair enough, but I don't see how a nose ring affects your work. Either way.

Mum and I were sharing a room in her house, and it's funny; I share a room with Nana and I don't mind that, but when I'm with Mum I usually wish I had more space to myself. But this time it was easier because of how Mum had put the room together. She'd pushed two mattresses together in one corner and covered them with some bright material, and she'd pinned more material to the walls to cover up the cracked plaster with another big bit draped over a rail in one corner, to hang our clothes behind.

I thought it looked absolutely excellent. Mum said it looked a bit like a flea market and she wrinkled up her nose, but I could tell she was pleased that I liked it. I loved lying in the middle of the dazzle of fabric, and sleeping next to Mum felt like a sleepover party, the sort you read about. And I did get some time to myself, because Mum came to bed ages after me. I could read in bed or write things in my notebook or just lie there and think, and leave the light on if I wanted to, which I can't do at Nana's. If I was still awake when Mum came in we talked, and first thing in the morning, too, before we got up. And it was good to have time together; she was right about that.

Mum's not comfortable talking to order, though. She never wants to answer direct questions, up front, about particular things. For instance, it's no good saying to her, *What happened about you breaking up with Dad? Do you ever think about him? Am I like him or more like you?* Or even, *How long will we stay here?* Because that doesn't work, she just slides out the side of the question and you find yourself talking about something completely different before you know it. If I want to talk to Mum about a particular thing I have to sneak up on it. I get started talking about something else, and when I think she feels relaxed, I come around to it from another direction.

But I didn't try that very much. Mum likes hearing about school, so I told her about Monica turning up. She likes Monica, they met before, and Mum said I should ask her back for tea. When I did, Monica latched right on to one of the two teenage boys who were in the house with their mum, although they had a room to themselves, of course. They were a first; there hadn't been kids older than me before in any of Mum's houses. These two go to high school so I didn't see much of them, but Zach—he's only two years older than me—was quite friendly sometimes. His brother, Josh, is a bit of a geek, but okay. Anyway, Monica and Zach hooked up and Mum thought I'd mind but I don't. Zach's nice enough; he even let me play around with his video games, which turned out to be more interesting than I thought. I don't fancy him, though. So far I only want to be friends with boys, not have boyfriends. Monica's ahead of me there.

The other people who live in the house seemed more or less okay, but I wasn't so sure about the hangers-on. Extra people often hang around the houses Mum lives in; people who don't rent rooms there, they just spend their days sitting around or even sleeping in empty beds. I've learned to check them out right from the start, and decide if I'm going to talk to them or keep out of their way. But in this house, Mum didn't let the hangers-on into our room. We kept the door locked when we were out, and I had a key on a wristband. I liked that, it was a sign that Mum and I shared something just between the two of us.

There was another good first: Mum liked her job! She said she enjoyed it instead of just enduring it. It was almost full-time in a fabric shop, so that's where the wall hangings and the bedcover came from. They couldn't easily sell left-over bits of fabric because they were too small for sewing, so Mum could take them home.

After a few days I got into the habit of going to Mum's shop after school to pick her up. The shop's called Material World, like that Madonna song, which is quite a cool name. Sometimes I stood out in the street for a few minutes and watched Mum through the shop window. One time she was serving a woman and her teenage daughter, and lifting these bolts of fabric off the shelves and shaking them out to show off the patterns. I could tell Mum really knew what she was doing, explaining the trick of sewing with this one or that one, and which fabric would hang best if you wanted to make a skirt, and which one would wash well if you needed it to. She was good at sewing, and that definitely helped her in the job.

When it was Mum's turn to cook, we'd walk home by way of the shops to buy food. The grown-ups took turns with the main meal, and when it was Mum's night we did it together. Mum cooked dinner soon after we arrived, and I made the lemon cake for dessert. The food Mum cooks is good, although it's a different style to Nana's. Mum mostly does vegetarian, which is ideal for her situation because some of the other people in the house don't eat meat, and it's easier to cook with them in mind than put together different meals. Nana likes veggies, she grows lots of them, but she doesn't serve them by themselves. That night Mum did a pumpkin risotto with a bit of cheese on top for protein, and a tomato salad to go with it. I've helped Mum make risotto before, and when I was little I used to sit on a stool by the stove and do the stirring for her. This time, though, I was busy making lemon cake.

It was still warm enough to eat on the front veranda, so we did. Zach and Josh carried out the big kitchen table and set up enough chairs. Robyn threw a spare curtain over the table and lit candles, and Amber picked bunches of leaves and grasses and put them around everyone's plates. There was wine for the grown-ups and apple juice or watered wine for the rest of us, depending on our ages and preferences. Mum's risotto was good, but I have to say that the dish of the evening was my lemon cake. Everyone loved it and wanted second helpings. Zach even licked the serving plate.

Mum seemed really happy, too. I watched her across

the table while the dishes were cleared away, which I didn't help with because it was a house rule that cooks didn't do that; all the others had to clear the table and do the washing up. Mum sat laughing and talking, and leaning back in her chair to call out to people in the kitchen. She seemed relaxed, and she wasn't drinking much, either. She'd only had one small glass of wine.

My hopeful happiness grew and stretched with the days.

Chapter Five

I phoned Nana at the end of the second week.

"I might stay on a bit longer than I said, if that's okay with you. Maybe closer to the school holidays."

"Things are good, then, eh?" The connection wasn't clear and her voice was a bit crackly, but she sounded fine. I couldn't remember her ever being sick, Nana didn't even get colds when everyone else was sniffing and sneezing. So I thought if she wasn't well I'd notice right off, even on the phone, because she'd be bound to sound different.

"They are. Honestly. Mum's got a job she likes, and she's happy. I'm happy, too. What about you?"

Nana's laugh came through the crackle.

"I'm fine, too, Jess girl. Never better. But missing you, eh? Missing you."

I hesitated. Maybe I should go back, anyway? Maybe Nana needed me? But the line suddenly cleared and her voice came through strong and clear.

"I don't mean you should come home, Jess girl. I can miss you without needing you to rush back, you know. You stay on a bit if you like, it's good for you to spend time with April, see more people your own age and enjoy city life as well. Watch TV, too, which I know you like to do. And school's okay, is it?"

I grinned into the phone. TV reception wasn't great at Nana's house because of the mountains, and she knew I liked to catch up with my favorite TV programs when I was in town. I hadn't mentioned Zach's video games to her, she'd only worry that I wasn't studying hard enough. And trust her to check up on school as well!

"School's good at this new place. We're doing lots of art, good stuff using things you find lying around, like you do with weaving. Shells and grass. And you'll like this one: We're using plastic bags!"

Nana laughed. "No shortage of those around! They're everywhere, up tall trees, even lying around in the bush. Dr. Gullick's adding them to the recycling plan." Nana and the local doctor are always nagging the council about recycling. They call themselves the Waimotu Wastebusters.

"Dr. Gullick would like my South African teacher," I said. "He calls our plastic-bag project 'creative recycling.' He got the idea from the townships where they make all kinds of things out of stuff no one else wants."

The project's like 3-D collage, only better. You shove as many plastic bags as you can onto an armature, like with papier-mâché. You squeeze all the bags on tight and you keep on going long after you think you can't squeeze one more on. Then you bend the whole frame around, and trim the bags, and—presto!—you've got an animal. I started with a chicken because I only had yellow plastic bags, and a few pink ones for a frill of neck feathers. If you had brown and black ones you could do a kiwi. I struggled to explain it all to Nana, but I was just making shapes in the air with my hands, and gave up.

"I'll bring you something I've done when I come back. You'll like it, Nana."

Nana always had stuff I'd made on display in the front room. She said she likes to study them at leisure while she's listening to the radio or her CDs. She brags about them to visitors, going on about how talented I am. I don't know about that, to be honest, but I enjoy making things. Wanting to do it is what makes the difference, I reckon, but Nana doesn't buy into that.

"She gets it from my side of the family," she says. "My own mother, she was a weaver. I keep that up as best I can but I haven't got a natural feel for it, the way she did. And now it comes out in Jessye, the artistic bent, eh?"

I don't know that it has to come from Nana's family, though, if I've got any talent to start with. Look at Mum and how she loves fabrics and all their colors and patterns, and how she sews and paints whenever she has the chance. Maybe that's what I inherited.

Mum had planned a whole lot of things for us to do together, just like she'd said. I hadn't been sure she'd meant it—well, she'd have meant it at the time she said it, but it might not have still been true when the time came around. Sometimes her plans never turn into reality. But she'd put a lot of thought into them this time, and I won't pretend I didn't like that. I loved it!

Her job ended early two days a week, so on those days she'd meet me after school and we'd go off on a mystery tour. One day we went down to the harbor and watched cargo boats unloading containers from around the Pacific, swinging them way over our heads on gigantic gantries. That might have been tedious after the first five minutes— but not with Mum. She invented a guessing game about what was in the containers, and adding them all together as a memory test. Once we got up to twenty-two things in a row, adding each unlikely thing to the one before. I really lost it when Mum added, "and seventeen thousand Barbie dolls," to my last item, which had been, "one, just one, but a very large one, banana." You get the idea, silly but fun.

Another time we walked down to the shoreline at low tide, and on around the rocks to a good sandy beach. Mum declared a handstand competition between the two of us, just because the sand was perfectly smooth and no one else had walked on it since the tide went out. She said, "We should celebrate this!" and so we did. I won at handstands, I'm good at them, but Mum won on turning cartwheels. She can do them for longer than me. In fact, she's so good she could be a professional cartwheeler if she chose, if anyone would pay you to do them, which I doubt. Then Mum pulled a surprise picnic from her backpack and we sat and ate and watched the shadows stretch out longer and darker while the sun dropped into the water. Not as good a sight as Waimotu, but choice in its own way.

Mum also discovered oil-painting classes at the local community center. It was called Paint Out because they held it out in the courtyard, and it was specially for family groups.

"That's us! That's you and me, Jayjay! We're a family group!" said Mum happily, signing us up. We both loved the smell of the oil paints as well as the way you spread them over the canvas and build them up. It was almost like a living thing, Mum said. I thought it was more like peanut butter and I wanted to squidge it around by hand, like with finger painting.

I tried painting the view from Nana's veranda. I like how you can make oil paint all shifty and glinting, like the river was in my memory, but I didn't do that good a job. Mum prefers painting people, and her picture of me was better than my river one. The teacher, Ted, loved her work and said Mum had the makings of a real artist, although you could tell he was only flirting with her; you couldn't believe anything he said. He even went on about her name—"April's such an *artistic* name for someone with your natural abilities," is only one of the dorky things he said to her. Mum flirted right back at him, looking sideways through her eyelashes and then dropping her gaze with a little smile: the whole bit. And then, as soon as she'd dropped her gaze and Ted had blushed and moved on, she'd look at me and roll her eyes. Mum didn't fancy him or even anything close to that, she just liked the classes. Ted, though, he just liked Mum.

Mum's very pretty; it's not just the art teacher who thinks so, everyone does. Lots of men fancy her. She's not very tall, and since I've grown recently we're almost the same height. But she has lots of curly blonde hair, and big eyes that are sometimes green and sometimes brown, depending on what she's wearing. Last year she had a habit of putting ribbons in her hair; she had different colors to go with her clothes, and Robyn used to sing a folksong to her—kind of teasing her, but in a good way. The song goes like this:

> *Her eyes they shone like diamonds*
> *I called her the queen of the land*
> *And her hair hung over her shoulders*
> *Tied up with a black velvet band.*

And the thing was, that suited her because Mum's eyes really do shine when she's happy, and her hair still hangs down over her shoulders, even now when she's given up the velvet bands. She has a great figure, too, curvy but not too curvy; she just goes in and out at the right places. And she wears skirts a lot—little short frilly ones—which look terrific on her. She's always on at me to wear skirts, too, but I'm not having it. She should know by now I don't like them on me.

I don't think I've inherited any of Mum's pretty bits, but the annoying part is, I don't seem to have inherited any of Nana's good bits, either. Nana's older than you'd think a beautiful person would be but she has great cheekbones, even Mum says that, and her skin's not saggy and her hair is shiny and wavy, even though she wears it in a braided bun most of the time so you can't really see it. I don't look much like either of them, which is disappointing. But there's still time for something good to develop.

Mum started talking about a trip for us at the start of the school holidays. "No tent this time, I swear, Jayjay!" she promised, and we both burst out laughing. Whatever happened, tent or no tent, we'd have a good time. I wasn't sure it would really happen, though, so I didn't mention it to Nana, not yet.

But if it did—well, it was a good reason to stay even longer.

It wasn't until I'd been with Mum for almost a month that anything began to go wrong. It started slowly, so I didn't notice the difference at first. It was only later, looking back, that I could see how things changed.

I do try to ignore the signs of anything going wrong when I'm with Mum. When I'm not with her, I think about her, of course, but I try not to worry. Sometimes I can't help it, but I do try. Because—well, because she's my mother and I love her. I hate to catch myself thinking things like: She shouldn't be doing that, or, How can I stop her doing it? or even just, I wish she wouldn't. Because it isn't any use. If I'm not there I can't help, and even when I am, I mostly can't help, either.

I hate to catch myself wishing she was different. Mum's how she is, and there's a really good side to her, and I should just get on with trying to accept that. Sometimes how she behaves makes me uncomfortable; it can even make me miserable, but I have to concentrate on the good things, and think about the Mum who says, "We owe it to ourselves to have fun, go on adventures and enjoy ourselves, Jayjay." I want to help her be more of that person, and less of the other one. But when the other one starts showing I don't know how to stop it.

Ages ago—it was after living in the bus with Mum had gone wrong and I was back at the river house with Nana—I tried to tell her that Mum would be fine if someone just gave her another chance. I don't know where I got the idea of "another chance" from, probably Mum. Anyway, Nana sat me down and took my hand in hers, and looked me straight in the eye.

"Jessye girl," she said firmly, "the thing about hope is, it's the hardest kind of loving you can do in this life. I'm not saying you shouldn't hope good things for your mum—you should; we all should, eh? We should all hope for good for one another, no matter what. But—" and then she squeezed my hand to make sure I was paying attention—"but hoping too much, for the wrong things, can break your heart. And if your heart breaks, my little mokopuna, well then mine will, too. For you."

I've never forgotten that. It didn't stop me hoping for good things for Mum, but it gave me a kind of shield against disappointment. Like in a song that Nana taught me for a concert around that time, which has a happy tune, although the subject is serious. The verse I'm talking about goes like this:

I'm going to lay down my sword and shield
Down by the riverside, down by the riverside,

I'm going to lay down my sword and shield
Down by the riverside,
I'm going to study war no more.

Nana explained what a shield was, and about what studying war meant. But I liked it because I always pictured the riverside in that verse being the one in front of her house.

This time, with Mum, the things that started to go wrong were the same old same old in one way, but different in another way.

The same old same old part was that Mum started to drink more, again. That's not easy for me to talk about. Admitting that something's the case doesn't mean you want to go on about it, and Mum often doesn't drink all that much.

Maybe just one glass of wine with her dinner, and then she stops. But I saw her glass was getting topped up a lot. She was even holding it out for more, please, which I hadn't noticed before.

It wasn't only Mum who was drinking more. Most of the grown-ups were doing it, but not everyone has Mum's problem. By the time I went to bed she was flushed and edgy, and not as relaxed as she had been. Little by little, she focused more on the next glass of wine that was coming along than on the company of her friends. Or on me, for that matter. She stopped planning a holiday trip, for instance; she even stopped making little teasing references to it to keep me interested. So I could tell it wasn't going to happen after all.

I'd been in that situation with Mum before, of course. Sometimes I feel mean about complaining, because it sounds as if I mind because of *me* and not her. But the truth is, when Mum's drinking she stops being my full-on mother. In my heart I know she still wants us to spend time together, but that part of her takes a backseat and she just isn't interested after all. Which is a bit like at school if your best friend stops being a friend, only it's worse than that because you can usually find new friends but you can't get another mother. Mum just wasn't watching and listening in the same way. Like I'm in another room, even when we're side by side, like there's an invisible wall between us.

I once tried to talk to Robyn about Mum's drinking, but Robyn closed down as soon as she got what I was saying. She said she didn't see a problem, that Mum drank a normal amount of wine—no more than other people. I reckon Robyn just didn't want to talk to me about it. I didn't think she believed what she was saying. How could she? She'd been around when Mum got sick from drinking too much, and even when she'd fallen over. She couldn't really think there wasn't a problem.

I didn't try talking to Robyn this time. She's a nice person, no mistake, but she's also a bit flaky. She's there for Mum when Mum needs her and that's a good thing, but Robyn doesn't go in for the hard things in life. It's like how she is with Amber. Amber's nice but she's pretty well spoiled. She gets away with almost everything and Robyn never calls her on it. It's easier not to, so she doesn't.

Chapter Six

Like I said, some of the troubles with Mum were the same old ones, but there were new ones, too. The main problem was that one of the hangers-on in our house was encouraging Mum to drink. At first I didn't blame him, because he wasn't exactly twisting her arm. But when someone like Adrian's around it's hard for Mum to stick at just one glass. Adrian was always there with a wine bottle, pouring out refills.

Adrian wasn't someone I'd decided to avoid—the exact opposite, in fact, which just shows how you can get sucked into someone's idea of themselves and be blind to the truth. He had a nice smile and he was easy company. He seemed friendly but not over-friendly, and he treated everyone in the house more or less the same. In fact, he acted like someone you'd want for a neighbor: not pushy, but helpful when you needed it. He even said he'd take on the overgrown back garden, and started clearing a patch of ground for growing vegetables.

I like veggie gardens. I do Nana's with her when I'm at

the river house, so I helped Adrian. We spent hours hoeing weeds and feeding the soil with compost, although looking back, maybe I did more work than he did. But we talked about what to plant and when, and what to do about slugs and snails, and whether you should plant what you liked eating, or just easy things to grow.

Adrian couldn't have found a quicker way into everyone's good books. When Robyn's younger sister left for the university, the other grown-ups invited Adrian to move into her empty room.

"It'll be brilliant to have another man around," Mum said when she kissed me good night. She was going to a movie with Robyn and her sister, who was leaving the next day. Zach's mum was babysitting me and Amber. "Do us all good, I reckon."

Mum cooked the "welcome to the house" meal for Adrian. She asked me to make Nana's lemon cake for it, because Adrian hadn't had it before. We worked in the kitchen together, Mum stirring a spinach and tomato mixture on the stove top while I checked the lemon cake in the oven, and got the lemon sauce ready for when the cake came out. I like the tomato and spinach thing of Mum's, and I've written down the recipe to try out on Nana. I'll need to take back a couple of special things, like a sheep's milk cheese called feta, which I haven't seen in Irma's shop in Waimotu. And fennel seeds, although maybe you could use wild fennel—it grows behind Nana's house.

"We're a good kitchen team, Jayjay," said Mum happily. "And we cook ace meals! We could open a restaurant together and charge top dollar!"

It made me happy to do stuff with her, and she seemed more like she had been just a few weeks earlier. It seemed a lot longer now.

I washed lettuce for Mum's salad and loaded it into the salad spinner. Then I ran outside to whirl the basket around my head and dry the leaves. It's got to be the most fun you could have with a salad, shaking out the basket and then spinning it around. Maybe I should get Nana a spinner to take back as a present. She just pats it dry on a tea towel, but the basket's a lot better. I walked back in thinking I'd suggest it to Mum; she might even help me buy one.

But when I went into the kitchen, Adrian was leaning against the stove, holding a bottle of wine and talking softly to Mum. He'd poured Mum a glass, and she was sipping as she stirred the food and listening to him. When I came in he stopped talking for a moment, and out of nowhere a cold splash of darkness touched me on the shoulder.

I don't know how else to describe it. The shiver went right down my arms; I almost dropped the spinner full of clean lettuce. It was like some sort of warning; a bit like a premonition, which is when you get a message from the future, but it was more like: *This is how he really is.* Or maybe even, *This is how they both really are.*

I tried to shake it off. *There's nothing wrong with them talking to each other,* I said to myself. *And it's only one glass of wine.* But even then I knew it wasn't just about Mum and a glass of wine. It was about Adrian, and how he'd stopped what he was saying when I came in.

The meal was fine, and everyone praised the cake again, but I kept worrying about Mum, and glancing at her through the meal, trying not to make it obvious. She was flushed and lively, and going off like a cracker in the conversation, telling jokes and stories and laughing at other people's, too—a bit too loudly, and a bit too long. And leaning in against Adrian to get another drink, and staying close to his shoulder even when her glass was refilled.

She'd had a lot to drink. Even I lost count of how many glasses she'd had, but I knew it was way too many. And I noticed that Adrian didn't drink much wine himself. He filled up the other glasses, but he hardly ever refilled his own.

"Time for bed, Amber," said Robyn. By then Amber and I were sitting on the veranda steps while Zach and Josh cleared up and washed the dishes (and moaned about it every step of the way, I have to say). I'd been excused because of the lemon cake, and Amber got off because, well, because she was Amber. She often slid out of her house jobs. No wonder the guys moaned, is one way to look at it.

"You, too, Jayjay," said Mum. Her words were slurred, and I glanced at Robyn to see if she'd noticed. She wasn't looking. By now Mum had moved her chair close to Adrian's, and they were talking just to each other; not the others.

And why not? I want her to have fun, don't I? No reason why not. She hasn't had a boyfriend in ages.

But in my heart I knew that things were going badly wrong. Knew it deep inside where the dark icy shiver had found a home.

Mum and Adrian became an item pretty fast after that. Mum still lived in our room but she stayed up late with him, and got up before me to have breakfast with him before she went to work and Adrian went off to—well, wherever. He didn't have a regular job—he did odd jobs; mostly other people's gardens, which is probably where he got the veggie plants he claimed he'd grown from seed.

I could tell that Mum was genuinely keen on him because she pretended she wasn't. When Mum has a boyfriend she's often funny with me about it. She used to try to keep it a secret, although I could mostly see for myself.

I don't know why she ever worried, I honestly don't mind, not usually, anyway. But this one was different. For starters, I couldn't see why she liked him. Adrian's not her usual type. His hair's thin on top and he's got a funny chin. Mum usually goes for fit types.

Also, Adrian wasn't a good bet because of the drinking. At first, I couldn't see why he encouraged Mum to drink. He mightn't have minded her getting drunk, although I couldn't see why he wouldn't. Mum's almost always fun, drunk or sober, but you'd have to think she was more fun when she wasn't slurring her words or repeating herself all the time, wouldn't you? But after awhile, I thought I saw a reason he could have, and it frightened me.

Mum isn't the same person when she drinks as when she's stone-cold sober. I like the stone-cold sober Mum best, but Adrian seemed to prefer the "agree to anything" Mum. And that's not good, because when things aren't going well for her, Mum sucks up crazy ideas in a heartbeat with no questions asked. I'm not talking about a way-out theory like aliens stealing human bodies. I'm just talking about money.

One time Mum joined one of those pyramid-selling schemes—bottled water with some special ozone added to it that was supposed to do you good. Mum had to sell cases of it but the scheme just sucked up all her savings. She had to buy so many cases to get started and she never earned enough to cover what she'd already spent on the water, let alone make a profit. And that was someone's great idea she'd taken up after she'd been drinking.

Another of her selling schemes was T-shirts door-to-door. People had to order their personalized T-shirts and got them delivered the next week. Mum drove miles trying to talk people into signing up for T-shirts in advance. She lost money on that, too, and we had cartons of T-shirts hanging around for months.

Now it was Adrian, always on at Mum about different ways to make money. He had a whole pack of ideas, and he'd circle around them, like a pig dog picking up scent in the bush. "Got to work out where the good money is," he said to Mum. His favorite idea was health drinks, and he said you had to invest in the company that made the drinks before you could get in on the act and sell stuff. Well, Joe once told me about a scam where a friend of his had lost his savings, and Adrian's health drinks, which were called New Way, sounded just like it. Even the name. I remember that Joe said, "New Way? No Way is what they should call it. Or an old way to part fools from their money." And why I even remember it is because then he said, "That company's as shady as a seven-dollar bill," which was funny. But I reckoned that Adrian might be shady, too, for all his smooth talk and smiles.

The next thing I heard from Mum was, she didn't like her job anymore! I knew that wasn't true, I'd seen her enjoying it with my own eyes, and I reckoned that Adrian was encouraging her to be unhappy. Mum said she liked serving customers but didn't like long stretches of time with nothing much to do. She liked sorting out the new orders when they arrived but she didn't like having to tidy the stockroom, which she said was "boring beyond bearing." She didn't like being sent out for cups of coffee by the owner, June, and she hated it when June took over a customer that Mum had started to serve. I have to say I was sympathetic about that; I wouldn't have liked it, either.

"It's not that I earn more money when I serve more people," Mum explained. "I mind because I like the contact with people, and it makes the day go quickly. Otherwise half the time I'm just staring into space imagining what clothes I'd make for myself from all that fancy fabric." Mum grinned at me when she said that, and turned to me instead of Adrian.

"And for you, too, Jayjay!" she added. "There's a pretty pink cotton on special offer that'd make you a lovely skirt."

"Mum! You know I hate pink, and I don't wear skirts," I said firmly. I had no intention of getting into girlie things to indulge Mum's fashion ideas, and her discontent bothered me. When I pushed her she admitted this was the best job she'd had in a long time. She even agreed that she liked going to Material World, despite the troubles, but all the good bits were being covered up by a rising tide of complaints. I told her it was like that for me at school, that I had to endure the classes I didn't like in order to get to the ones I did enjoy, and I could see she understood what I meant.

Adrian listened to me without disagreeing. He didn't actually say anything at all. But when I'd finished, he just turned back to Mum and started talking about New Way again. So I hadn't won the point after all. Not with either of them.

That night when I was getting ready for bed, Mum said, "He's really nice, isn't he?" I knew she meant Adrian. I mumbled something into the shirt I was pulling over my head, and the moment passed, which was lucky. I didn't think I should say, *No, he isn't.*

For one thing, there's not much to put your finger on with him, apart from things that I can't easily say to

Mum. Like, for instance, *No, because he helps you drink too much,* or, *No, because he's got these bad ideas about money and get-rich-quick schemes.* Or, *No, because I had a cold rush of fear when I saw him with you in the kitchen.* How mad would that sound?

And I don't know—but Mum looked so happy when she said that about him being nice. I didn't want to spoil it for her, either.

I began to wish I was back with Nana so I didn't have to deal with all the hassle. I'd started sleeping badly again, and I couldn't get back to sleeping right through the night. And I missed Nana a lot after the first weeks. Little things would happen and I'd think, I must tell Nana that, or, That would make Nana laugh. But I knew that I couldn't talk to her about the problems with Mum. I already knew what she'd say about the drinking, so what was the point in troubling her? How she felt was more or less how I felt, too, but there was always one important difference: I loved Mum, anyway, whatever she did, and Nana didn't.

Nana didn't think I should be responsible for Mum; she'd say that Mum had to be responsible for herself— "She's a grown-up, Jessye girl," was her line. "She's an adult and you're not. And no matter how grown up you act on occasions you're still young, not even a teenager yet. That's the difference right there, and it's a whole world of difference, too. You can't be responsible for her—you can only try to be responsible for yourself. You can't change April, you know, girl. No one else in the world can do that.

Only she can change, if she chooses." Which is all very well, but if I didn't help, who would?

If I told Nana about Mum's drinking she'd want me to come home on the next bus, and leave Mum to it. She might even come up and take me back with her; she'd done that once before when I was little, when she hadn't been able to get through to Mum on the phone for days. She'd taken one look at how things were, and scooped me back to Waimotu with her. I didn't see Mum for almost a year after that.

I didn't think Nana'd do the same thing now, but I didn't want to risk a fuss. And I also thought that, just on this one thing, Nana might be wrong. But all the same, just the thought of Nana was turning into a longing for her company, for the house and the river, and for my life when I was there. Even a longing for Tu, who I didn't exactly bond with.

Nana could sense something was wrong when I phoned, though. I always just chatted away about all the good things I could think of—little things that Amber and I had done together, and about Monica, and what was happening in town. But she could tell something was up. She'd have guessed it was to do with Adrian, because I'd mentioned him and said he was Mum's new boyfriend, and Nana probably thought I was jealous of him.

I decided to leave everything for one more week. Maybe Mum's job would improve or she'd feel better about it; maybe Mum and Adrian might get less friendly of their own accord. Maybe Mum would just settle back down again. So I decided to keep my head down and concentrate on school.

What is it with resolutions, anyway? The moment you get to a decision about what to do—well, the very *next* moment is when something else happens to change your whole thinking. And the night after I'd decided to keep my head down for a while, that's when Adrian started quizzing me about Nana.

When we worked on the veggie garden together, Adrian always asked me tons of questions. At first, I reckoned he was just being polite, keeping the conversation moving along the way grown-ups do, and I didn't know any better than to answer him.

I'd said what Nana grew in her veggie plot; how she started off her leek plants; how Swiss chard could keep you going right through the year if you got the planting right, and how arugula self seeded so you never had to buy more seeds, it came up everywhere whether you wanted it or not. And he must have worked out other stuff while I talked; things I hadn't spelled out, and didn't mean to say. Or maybe Mum told him things. I didn't remember mentioning Uncle Joe, for instance, but Adrian was even nosy about him. Did Joe call around to Nana's a lot, or only when she asked him to? Did Joe advise her about her money; he was a money man wasn't he, doing books and keeping accounts for a living, wasn't that true?

None of your business, is what I thought, and he

hadn't even finished asking. How long had Nana lived in the river house? Was it hers? Did she own all that land? Or did it belong to someone else?

"What the heck is all this? What do you want to know for?" I blurted that out and I admit it sounded rude. Right away, Adrian's expression of lively interest changed to irritation, like he resented being thwarted. I'd not seen him drop his nice face before and it was a pity Mum didn't see the change, but she'd turned to look at me in surprise. Then she leaned forward and tapped my hand.

"There's no call for rudeness. Answer Adrian's questions, Jessye," she said quietly but firmly. She almost never called me by my full name, only when she was cross. I didn't want her to be. If she was cross or anxious she might drink more to calm herself, or start up again about not liking her job, so I had to be careful.

"Actually, I meant to say, what exactly do you want to know first?" I lied, smiling brightly at Adrian. "What in particular, I mean. Lots of questions there, Adrian!" He smiled back, pacified, but more cautious.

"Your grandmother owns her own property, that's right?" he asked. I nodded. "And it's hers?" he continued. I nodded again because I thought that was true. Nana always talked about it as if it belonged to her.

"And—it's Maori land? So it can't be sold to just anyone, is that right?"

"I think so," I answered. "I don't know for sure, but I think so."

Mum leaned forward again. She'd been watching the two of us in turn as we spoke, like we were batting a ball back and forth.

"Jessye's her grandmother's only grandchild," she added, surprising me. Why would Mum want to tell anyone that? "Probably her only heir as well," she added.

I half rose from my chair in protest. "Mu-um! Please don't!" I felt myself blushing. I didn't want just anyone to talk about me and Nana like that. It was private business. Family business. Adrian wasn't family.

He will be family, though, if he and Mum stay together. The thought ran through my mind like a ripple, but I pushed it away.

Mum looked surprised. "Well, but it's true, Jessye," she said. "Your grandmother's worth a lot of money, if she ever wants to do anything with it." She turned to Adrian. "Mina gave some land to Joe when he got married," she added. "She's still got a lot left, though."

I knew that was right about Joe's property. His land runs with Nana's along the back hill, so he doesn't have the river, but he's got an awesome view from his front porch because he's up on the ridge. But I didn't want to talk about it with Adrian.

"Nana's worth a lot, money or no money!" I said hotly. "You can't put a value on her!" The conversation was starting to frighten me.

"Just a value on her property," Adrian corrected smoothly. "No one's trying to put a money value on a human life, Jessye. We know you love your grandmother."

Mum shifted in her seat, leaned over to tidy up some crumbs on the tabletop. Busy work, I thought to myself. Mum never minds about crumbs or tidying up unless she's trying to distract herself from something else.

"I'd like to talk to her about it," Mum said carefully after another pause. She didn't look at me; she looked down at the crumbs she'd tidied together in a little pile in front of her plate.

"The thing is, Jayjay," she said, and stopped again. There was a pause while Mum fiddled some more with the crumbs.

"Say your grandmother wanted to invest in something. She could use her land to raise money; she wouldn't have to sell it first, or anything like that."

I didn't answer. There was another pause, another pass at the crumbs.

"Do you think she'd—that maybe you could—" Mum stopped to glance up again and check my response. I kept my face as still as I could, although my heart and mind were racing away. I just looked back at her, waiting for the worst.

Mum shrugged, got up, and started clearing the table.

"Another time," she said to no one in particular. "I'll talk to you about this another time."

About Nana's money.

Did Adrian and Mum want to get some money out of her?

Or—even worse—did they want me to get some money from her?

I wouldn't do it. Couldn't do it. And I didn't want them to ask me to, either.

I helped Mum with the dishes, and at first there was an awkward silence between us. But when I switched on the radio to cover up the awkwardness, well, there it was. They were playing our song!

The thing is, there's a song that Mum made up, and she uses it when we've had a fight. I use it on her sometimes, too. It goes to the tune of "Release Me" but we have different words. So when that song was on the radio at that moment we looked at each other in disbelief, and burst out laughing. And then, of course, we started to sing along with the tune, but singing our words. It put us right back into harmony with each other. Our words go like this.

(Mum): Please, dear Jessye, don't be mad!
I hate it when you're cross with me or sad!
(Me): Okay, dear Mum, let's kiss and hug!
(Both of us): Let's stay together—warm and snug.

When I look at the words in my notebook I can see they're a bit pathetic. But when we sing them together, it's good fun. Anyway, right after that the radio went into a salsa program, so then Mum and I danced around while we put the dishes away. And Adrian came in and watched us, grinning, which was okay until he opened his mouth.

Because what he said was, "You two! What are you? That isn't by any chance the happy tent dance I heard about, is it? It looks like some sort of a haka, not that girls do war dances."

Which was about as far away from okay as you could get without starting to come back again. Because Mum and I *promised* each other we'd never mention the tent to anyone. I didn't like it that she'd mentioned the happy dance, but the tent story as well? I felt angry and sad all over again. Even the fact that Adrian got it wrong—like, it wasn't a happy tent dance, for pity's sake—didn't make it any better. Mum had told him about it and he'd just remembered it a bit wrong, but he still thought he could mention it.

Mum didn't even look ashamed. I don't know which was worse.

And saying that about a haka? That women don't do them? It just shows what he doesn't know, because they do. And if he saw women doing one, a proper women's haka, he'd probably die of fright.

Oh, you can say I was being babyish if you want to. But I was there, and I know how it was. I don't think it was right or fair what she'd done.

Chapter Seven

The very next day at school, an amazing thing happened. Lovey turned up! Monica and I were on our way to the art room at morning break and there she was, waiting in the corridor outside the principal's office. She was looking nervous, not like the confident chat-to-anyone Lovey I knew from Waimotu, but it was her all right. My mouth dropped open like someone in a cartoon strip; I sort of gawked at her in surprise, so when she saw me she started giggling instead of joining me in the *Can-it-be-you? Surely-not? Oh, wow!* routine that I launched into.

I was so pleased to see her again. It was like having family around. Lovey's part of my whanau, my family group, so somewhere down the line we share the same ancestors. We're cousins, really, so we call each other "cuzzie" sometimes. When I'm with Mum I don't usually see my Maori family, and when I'm with Nana I don't usually see Mum and her friends. Mum doesn't have close family, because she never had brothers or sisters and her parents are dead. So strictly speaking there's only me in her family, but she always says her friends are her family, next in line to me.

Anyway, that's why seeing Lovey was special. It was a bit like mixing up the pieces of two separate jigsaws and discovering you could construct a new picture that way; one to suit the whole of you.

The school secretary whisked Lovey into the office before we could talk, and I didn't see her again until after lunch. I hoped she'd be put in my class but she went into Ms. Matia's class down the corridor from mine. Luckily we were together for gym, so we ended up on the same softball team in the afternoon. And when it was our turn to play the outfield we stood as close together as we could, without attracting attention from the teachers and being told to spread out.

"What are you doing here?" I called over to her. Lovey grinned back at me.

"Could ask the same thing of you, Jessye Cooper!" she said. Lovey's voice is the sort that carries over distances without her having to shout; it's low but it's clear. She'd probably be good at the waiata tawhito, the old songs you chant instead of singing. I planned to mention that to Nana when I saw her; she'll probably say something to Lovey's family and get her learning them. Anyway, Lovey said that her dad, who's a lawyer, was off in Wellington for a court case. So she and her mum were staying with an auntie over our side of town, because her mum needed help with her new baby.

"And I'm staying with my mum for a while," I explained. Lovey raised her eyebrows at me and I could understand why she would, even from across the softball field. Lovey would think I'd rather be with Nana any day, because the one thing she knew about me for sure, what I'd told her, was how much I liked living in the river house. And she'd never met my mum.

I had a strange moment then, while I was waiting for someone to hit the ball in our direction. I got a kind of flash—the clearest picture of Nana and the river house—but it wasn't like a memory or a movie; I could *see* it in front of me. The wide shimmer of water, and the sweep of hills over on the far side. I could even smell the mangrovey air. It was as clear as the softball field, and as sharp as the thwack of the ball on the bat. I could have turned around and touched Nana because I knew she was standing beside me, looking at the same thing. And then it melted away and I was on the field at school, blinking in the sunlight.

It could have been a scary experience, but actually it felt okay. But it also reminded me of Lovey's taniwha story, because Nana and I had been watching something in the river and right away, I thought of the taniwha. There was no chance to quiz Lovey then; we had to change sides and line up to bat. And it wasn't something to rush at. I wanted to sit her down and get her to tell me everything she knew.

So a couple of days later, after school, we went back to Lovey's mum's auntie's house. Lovey's mum was always laughing and telling jokes when I met her in Waimotu—like Lovey, only more so. Now she was sleepwalking through the day because Moana, the new baby, was hardly sleeping at all, but she still gave me a welcome. She acted surprised, though, that I was in town instead of with Nana.

Like Lovey, she probably thought I'd rather be at the river house than anywhere else, so why wasn't I, kind of thing. People often don't understand why I'd be with Mum, but anyone who knows her like I do can see why I'd want to spend time with her.

Moana is as cute a baby as I've ever seen; she's got lots of curly dark hair already, even though she's only new, and her eyes are enormous, just like Lovey's. Lovey and I tickled her fat little tummy and made her smile, although Lovey said it was wind, not smiles, and that her tummy hurt, which was why she wasn't sleeping. Lovey knows lots about babies because her bit of the family's always producing new ones. She knows how to pick them up and soothe them and change their diapers, and all that.

And then suddenly Moana went to sleep. One minute she was awake and the next minute—wham! out for the count. We put her down in her cot and then Lovey had to help her mum, so the two of us sat on the back step, stripping the silk from a bucket of sweet corn from the garden and talking, talking, talking. We stayed there long after the sweet corn was ready, until it was almost time for everyone to eat. I didn't stay for tea that night but I went back to Lovey's lots after that. It was open house at mealtimes and people just turned up, mostly with food to offer, and everyone who was there got fed. Which in one way is like being with Mum, that happens in her houses, too, but it's also so, so different.

The people arriving at Lovey's mum's auntie's house aren't like Mum's hangers-on. It's mostly a family connection that brings them, and like on the marae you have to figure out what the connection is. Sometimes I had a hard job following everything because people spoke more Maori than I was used to, and I felt shy about it. But there was always enough space for everyone, even if we had to set up a card table at the end of the big one, or feed the little kids first. Best of all, the food reminded me of Nana's meals. Big piles of veggies and help yourself to everything, but starting off with a thank-you prayer for having good things to eat, just like Nana does. It's called a karakia; they even do more or less the same one as Nana. It goes like this in Maori:

> *E te Atua*
> *Whakapaingia i enei kai,*
> *hei oranga mo o matou tinana.*
> *Amene.*

And in English it's this:

> *Dear Lord*
> *Please bless this food,*
> *which gives us life.*
> *Amen.*

When Lovey was around I saw more of her, and less of Monica. Not that Monica minded, because she was totally wrapped up with Zach now. Most days after school she'd be off on the bus to hang around the high school, and wait for him to come out.

And Lovey's taniwha story? I finally persuaded Lovey to tell me what she knew.

Sometimes it's hard to know where a story actually begins, and most Maori stories start way back in time. They might seem to be about the here and now, but most of them have their roots in the old days and the old stories. So you just have to dive in somewhere and start telling it your way, like Lovey did with hers.

Lovey said she'd been told there had always been a taniwha in Nana's river. She'd been told it had got lost in the river and couldn't find its way home, so it ended up living under the riverbank across from Nana's house.

For hundreds of years, this particular taniwha was happy enough in the river, tucked away under the bank in the middle of the mangroves. But something made it angry—no one knew what had upset it, Lovey said—and it remembered how it had got lost, and got miserable all over again. So it decided to take out its unhappiness on someone; make a human person sorry they'd ever been born.

Taniwha, they're not to be messed around with. They can travel around the underground waterways and pop up wherever they choose—in two places at once if they've a mind to, they're so big. One taniwha can be breathing out hot springs from its nostrils in one place, and lashing up a storm with its tail in another place that's maybe tens of kilometers away. Another famous taniwha guards the mouth of our river where it meets the open sea. If that one doesn't want you to get across the harbor bar it'll lash up a storm of rough water and capsize your boat in a flurry of foam. And if it doesn't like you; if you haven't done the right things to appease it, it'll even try to kill you. They're strong, stronger than anything else, with supernatural strength that no one can measure, so any one of them is a lot more powerful than any human. Taniwha might decide to be on your side if they choose, and if they are then you've got their magic on your side as well as good luck. But you shouldn't think that having such a creature on your team's going to make your life easy or straightforward. It could just make things worse.

I've always thought that taniwha might look a bit like dragons, but I imagine them covered with ta moko, tattoo patterns, from head to tail. And I know a joke about dragons that sounds right for the taniwha that Lovey was describing, the one in our river. It goes like this:

Do not meddle with the affairs of dragons,
for you are crunchy
and taste good with ketchup.

Lovey had to stop her story in mid flow when it was time to eat. She hadn't got to the bit about the flood and about someone drowning, and there was also the part about my dad to come. I didn't mind waiting, though. You don't necessarily mind not knowing something right off if you're not sure whether it's good or bad.

"You're Mina's mokopuna?" Lovey's own nana asked me at dinner that night. I nodded, proud that she knew I was Mina Cooper's granddaughter and happy to be noticed because of it. No doubt about it, it gave me something to live up to.

"You're as welcome as the sunshine," she said. Then she looked at me closer, in a sort of measuring way.

"Now, Jessye, are you like Mina, eh?" she asked. I thought she just meant did I have Nana's artistic talents, which I didn't want to claim for myself. So I just smiled back at her and said, "I hope so," which seemed to be enough.

"And how is she, your nana?" she asked gently.

"She's good," I said. "I talked to her last night. She told me . . ." I hesitated, trying to think of the Maori words for what I wanted to say. But Lovey's nana nudged me, smiling. "Go on," she encouraged. "Say it your way." She knew why I'd been shy.

"She said she was happy that I was spending time with my people," I said. "But I don't know for sure—are you whanau or hapu?" Lovey's nana threw back her head and cackled with laughter. That's where they get it from, Lovey and her mother, all those giggles.

"It's both of them, girl!" she told me. "We're whanau *and* hapu!"

And when I thought about it, I did understand. Maori family starts with your iwi—your tribe. And then it's your canoe, your waka, and who else traveled in that with your ancestor. After that it's your clan, your hapu, and finally it's your whanau, your family group. Lovey's people are part of all of those, so we share aunts and uncles and I don't know what else. Nana once said to me how terrific it was to hear someone saying their mihimihi on the marae and you suddenly realize—goodness! He's one of mine! It was like that.

When Lovey finally got to the bit about the drowning, and about my dad, it was more, and less, than I'd expected.

It was less, because the story wasn't finished. It didn't have a proper ending because Lovey said no one knew anymore; she'd asked around and they'd told her all they knew. "My mum, her sister, and my nana—they all said the same thing," she told me. "I can't tell you more than they told me."

This is what she said.

"About fifteen years ago, something like that, before we were born, anyway—that was the last time the river flooded over its banks. A huge storm surge of water up from the sea, salty and cold, saltier than normal. My auntie said even the mangroves didn't like that much salt in their lives, and they're used to salty water. And when it happened, the homes along the river got flooded out. They got water up over the floors; even way up the walls, because the houses sat so low to the ground."

I stopped her there, because there aren't any other houses close to Nana's on the river. Joe's house is up the hill, and there's no one else along the river until you get to the shops and the pub a couple of kilometers on down the road. So I wondered again, was this about Nana's place, or some other river?

But Lovey said she'd been told there had been houses

down by the river in Waimotu. And people had to leave them in a panic when the river rose. Everything they'd left behind had been lost to the floodwaters, and the houses were so badly damaged they'd been abandoned. And I suddenly remembered something I'd not thought about for years. It meant it could be true, after all.

Nana and I used to walk down the riverbank when I was little. We'd end up at Joe's place—you can get to him the long way around if you go along the bank and then up to the ridge. We'd pick wild plants that were good to eat, or Nana'd pull up tall fronds of flax and show me how to strip them and braid little baskets. I made one for Mum that she still has, even though the corners have frayed and it wasn't that neat to start with.

Anyway. One time I'd seen a pile of old bricks and a piece of corrugated iron crumbling into the gorse bushes by a tangle of blackberry bushes, a little way back from the bank. Nana told me it was all that was left of the chimney and roof of a house. Next time I looked, the bricks had gone. Someone must have taken them for another building. But the corrugated iron was still lying there, blooming with rust and lichen.

And that finally proved it in my mind. Now I knew Lovey was talking about the right place.

Lovey described how the people who'd lived in the little houses left when the waters kept rising. Everyone got away with their babies and dogs, and even with a few precious things they'd grabbed up as they ran. It all happened in the dark; just before dawn was what Lovey said, and in the middle of a fierce storm as well. I imagined how they'd have felt, stumbling around with the wind shrieking at them and the waters rising. It made me shiver in the sunlight, just thinking about it.

If Nana didn't like wild water, maybe that's where it started.

After everyone reached shelter, the men went back to rescue more things. But the storm surge was pulling back down the river by then, with the outgoing tide, and one of the men slipped and fell under the water. He'd been swept away by the current, and no one could save him. Drowned, though his body had never been found.

"And that's why people mention the taniwha," Lovey said. "Because of the body never turning up. They say the taniwha took him for company and kept him in a cave under the bank. They say he can't leave, not without the taniwha's permission. It wants company, and so he's stuck there underneath the bank. Singing songs to it, telling stories maybe, whatever, I don't know how he entertains it day after day for all this time. Sounds like *The Arabian Nights* to me. You know those stories?"

I did know. They're in a book, and a woman tells the stories every night to this man who's going to kill her. She leaves the ending open, up in the air, so each night he spares her life until the next day, so he can hear how that one ends. And so on, for a thousand and one nights. I wondered how many nights the man in Lovey's story had been held by the taniwha—by now it'd be more than a thousand and one.

"And the man—that was Hemi," said Lovey. I frowned; I'd heard that name somewhere.

"Hemi was the middle one of your grandmother's boys," Lovey went on. "So he's your uncle, Jessye, like Joe. Well, he *was* your uncle. He lived in one of those houses, and he's the one who drowned. Or the one the taniwha's kept for company . . ." Her voice trailed off.

"Hemi." I said the name out loud again. Lovey glanced at me.

"Hemi. So it's James, in English, but my mum called him Hemi."

I *had* heard about him. Not for ages, but when I was little, Nana had talked about him a bit. She'd told me what he was like when he was a baby; said he was a lot like me in his nature, and we liked doing things the same way—too fast, always rushing. I'd forgotten.

"So it was Hemi and Joe and my dad?"

"The third son's your dad, Michael." Lovey hesitated but I took no notice.

"Mikey." I liked to say his name out loud; sometimes I even said it to myself, when no one was around.

"Yeah, Mikey," Lovey repeated.

Joe, Hemi, and Mikey.

Three brothers.

"Mum said they were called the sons of thunder," she said, smiling wickedly at me. I didn't understand.

"Like in the Bible," Lovey prompted. "Two of the disciples, they were brothers? James and John, I think? Anyway, they were called the sons of thunder."

I didn't get it. "Why thunder, though, for Nana's boys? Okay, there might have been a James, but there wasn't a John. What's thunder got to do with it?"

Lovey laughed.

"It's not *what*, it's *who*! And the answer to *who* was the thunder—that was your nana! People called the boys the sons of thunder because they were so lively and loud, but in the end they reckoned your nana was the thunder—always sounding off!"

Lovey quickly added that she didn't mean any disrespect, it was just that Nana had strong opinions and wasn't slow to come out with them. I didn't mind, and, anyway, I was still concentrating on the boys.

"What else do you know about them? When they were our age?"

Lovey thought for a moment.

"I think Mum said they had a band. Country music, would that be right?"

I nodded, thinking about all Joe's country songs.

"Mum said they used to do an act together when they were teenagers, play their guitars and sing at parties." She smiled again. "And my nana said they used to bring the house down with one song, not a dry eye left in the room is what she said. It's just one of those songs that tugs at your heart."

I didn't know which song she meant until she hummed the tune, and then I recognized it right off. It's a famous tearjerker, and even if you don't want to cry when you hear it, it's very hard to stop yourself. It's called "Two Little

Boys"; Rolf Harris used to sing it. It's about two guys who've been friends forever, they're even maybe brothers. They share their toys, like a wooden horse, when they're kids, and look out for each other. And then they grow up, and they're soldiers in a battle, and one of them's wounded and dying. He's even called Joe, so you can see why the brothers might have liked singing it. Anyway, one of the verses goes like this:

> *Did you think I would leave you dying*
> *When there's room on my horse for two?*
> *Climb up here, Joe, we'll soon be flying*
> *Back to the ranks so blue.*
> *Do you know, Joe, I'm all a-tremble,*
> *Perhaps it's the battle's noise—*
> *But I think it's that I remember*
> *When we were two little boys.*

I thought about that for a while, and about Joe and Hemi and Mikey. Joe didn't sing that song anymore; I'd never heard him, anyway. You can see why not. I asked Lovey for anything else about my dad but she shrugged and said she didn't know.

"No one talks about him," she said. "My mum just says, 'He's gone from our sight.'" Which is like what I heard Nana saying to Joe. Talk about toeing the line.

I turned back to Lovey.

"But, Lovey, what about the taniwha?"

Lovey went serious again.

"Did you know that they were all there when Hemi drowned? Joe and Mikey almost drowned, too, trying to rescue him. And it's not over. People say, maybe the taniwha likes Hemi's company and wants more of the family, too? Or, this was from my nana's friend, she said there's unfinished business between your family and the taniwha, and that the taniwha owes your family a favor."

Then she shrugged again.

"Who knows, Jessye? It's only a story, not even a proper one with a beginning, a middle, and an ending."

But I thought she was wrong about that. I thought the story did have a beginning and end, even if we didn't know what they were. And the pair of us, sitting on the step? Well, destiny had dumped us both right in the middle of it. Or dumped me there, anyway, and since Lovey was family she was in it, too.

Chapter Eight

I've tried to find out more about my dad before. On the marae there's always someone you can talk to about the people who aren't there, as well as the ones who are. And I overheard a few secrets when I was little just by sitting quietly on the floor listening to the grown-ups talk, before they remembered I was there. And once or twice someone started saying something about Nana's boys. They'd lean forward and lower their voices, and I'd lean in a bit and hope to hear something. But their eyes would slide sideways, back to me and then on to wherever Nana was, and even if she wasn't looking our way they'd sit back again and change the subject, or ask me to get them another cup of tea or more cake.

I always thought news about my father would come one way or another if I was patient. Like—oh, like maybe he'd gone to Australia, or he had a new life somewhere. Sometimes I imagined going to see him; I usually invented a long bus ride for myself and finally getting to a town, and there he'd be, waiting for me. I'd love to have brothers and sisters so I used to add little children to the picture, clinging on his shoulders or shy around his legs. And a new wife who'd be glad to have me help look after them.

I thought he'd be keeping an eye on me in some secret way. Maybe Joe would be telling him about me, because even though they'd fallen out they were still brothers. Joe wasn't that good a choice, though, because of not going against Nana. All Joe'll let himself do is have different opinions from her. So he scoffs at things like taniwha stories, and he cooks ready meals in a microwave. He says, give me the modern world and the more of it the better. He doesn't even recycle!

In my heart, I accept that my dad mightn't have kept up with me at all. If he had, someone would most probably have let something slip. But even so, you have to hope. And sometimes I still did.

That night I dreamed about Nana and the river.

I don't often remember my dreams, although Mum's into dreams in a big way. She says that's how hidden parts of our minds tell us important things, and we should use that knowledge in our everyday lives. She often nags me to tell her my dreams first thing in the morning, so she can have a go at interpreting them. Sometimes I make them up, so she won't go on at me to remember.

Nana doesn't think about dreams in the same way, but she says you should attend to them, especially if they stick in your mind. In my opinion, Mum's interest in dreams isn't exactly crazy but I don't agree with her about them. Or at least I didn't use to; maybe I'll change my mind now. Because this one was very scary.

It started in a familiar way, like an ordinary day. I often have dreams like that. I was standing on the front veranda of the river house looking out at the river, and it felt good, like wishing I was there.

But then, suddenly, there was a huge splash from the river and before I could see what had made the noise, Nana was beside me. She grabbed my hand and swung me around to look at her. And she said, "Don't look! Whatever you do don't look, Jessye girl!" And I suddenly knew that the two of us were in the most terrible danger. I even had that same cold shiver of fear I'd felt in real life with Mum and Adrian. And I tried to pull away from Nana, but her hand turned into a long snaky sort of tentacle covered in shiny stuff, like glue. It was disgusting and I screamed and tugged away even harder, and I was shivering and soaked in river water from head to foot. I heard Nana again, but this time her voice terrified me, because it came from inside the tentacle.

I thought the tentacle had eaten her. I was yelling things like "*No!*" and "*Get away!*" and "*Leave her alone!*" And the tentacle voice said something in Maori that I didn't understand, not then, anyway, but when I woke up I remembered the words, and then I did know what they meant.

It sounded like:

To Po nui!
Te Po roa!
Te Po kerekere!

I know those words from listening to Nana tell me stories, because it's the way the creation story starts in Maori and she's recited that to me tons of times. It's a bit like the one in the Bible, because it starts with the time when there wasn't any light, only darkness, in the whole world. The Maori words mean something like this:

The great night!
The long night!
The night of deep shadows!

That part of the story's pretty long but I remember the start; it goes like this:

Te Po nui
Te Po roa
Te Po uriuri
Te Po kerekere
Te Po tiwha
Te Po tangotango
Te Po te kitea.

It doesn't sound so impressive in English, and not so

frightening, either; I reckon you need the sound of the Maori words. Anyway, this is how I think it goes:

The great night!
The long night!
The dark night
The night of deep shadows!
The gloom-filled night
The night to be felt
The night unseen.

See? Not as good.

I woke up cold and shivering from being soaked in river water, but, of course, that was the dream, I was actually warm and dry and tucked up next to Mum. I must have shouted out loud because Mum turned over, the whole little cocoon of her and her blankets, and said, "Are you okay, Jayjay?" in a sleepy murmur, and sank back into sleep without waiting for me to answer. But the next morning when I got ready for school, Mum was waiting in the kitchen, with toast ready for me and a big glass of guava juice poured out. She hadn't done any of that in awhile.

"What was your dream about last night?" she asked me with a lively look on her face.

I told her some of it. I didn't say how frightened I'd been because I didn't want to remind myself about that. But I told her what the tentacle had said; I wanted to know what she thought.

Mum stirred her coffee slowly while she listened, looking

fascinated. I even spun the story out to keep her interested, although a bit of me despised myself for being so pathetic.

"The dream's telling you about your grandmother," she announced when I'd finished. "Mina's being pulled down under the water into a long, dark night. It's because she's not well, and she's telling you she wants you to help her." Mum put down her cup and touched me on the shoulder—a kind of *this is a special moment* touch.

"I want that, too, Jessye," she said excitedly. "I've been longing to talk to you about this. And now—well, this is a sign!"

I had a fearful moment of knowing that the dream was real and true. Like a sort of parallel universe thing. *Earth to Jessye*. And for a moment dark water surged around me again, and I had to shake my head to get myself back into the morning where Mum was, still going on about her idea.

"I think it's clear that your grandmother's not well, Jayjay," said Mum, leaning forward. "I said so in Waimotu— I tried to, anyway, but you didn't believe me. I had another go the other evening, but it made you unhappy so I didn't push it. But I want us to talk about it now if you'll let me."

Mum hadn't tried to talk about Nana's health the other night! She'd tried to talk about Nana's *money*! Was she really pretending that it had been different?

"Will you let me?" Mum persisted. I managed a nod in reply.

"Your nana, there's something wrong with her blood," Mum said in a low, important voice. Like she was saying, *The world is coming to an end and only I know about it*. That sort of voice.

How could Mum know such a thing when it was news to me? Why would Nana tell her and not me?

Nana had something wrong with her blood?

"I know!" It was like Mum had just read my mind. "Why should I know something like that when Mina would never tell me anything about herself that mattered?" She sat back in her chair and sipped her coffee, and then looked at me again.

"I've known it before, is how I can recognize it now," she added. "I've seen people with this trouble in their blood before, so I know what I'm talking about."

"What trouble?"

"I think it's an illness called leukemia, Jayjay." And she patted my hand again and explained that was a sickness when your blood didn't have the right number of white cells and red cells. Too many of one and not enough of the other; I'm not sure which because I didn't take it all in.

And when I asked, couldn't it be cured? Mum sighed and said yes, if you caught it in time, but she was willing to bet that Nana hadn't even told a doctor let alone had treatment, so what were her chances of getting better?

I started to feel panicky, even though I didn't trust the way she was talking about it.

"How can you know? How can you be sure?"

But Mum said she'd known as soon as she'd seen Nana

on her last visit; known without a shadow of doubt is what she said, and that she didn't need a doctor's verdict to confirm that.

By then I'd had enough, and I told Mum straight out that I didn't believe her. She got really sniffy—I knew she would—and then she stopped talking altogether.

The trouble was, when I thought about it more I saw that it could be true. Not that I was going to admit that to Mum. But I remembered how Lovey, and her mum, and her mum's auntie—they all asked me why I wasn't with Nana. Did they know, too? Is that why they'd asked me how she was and why I wasn't with her? Did everyone but me know that Nana was sick?

I didn't think Mum would straight-out lie to me about something so serious. But she might bend the truth if she was pushed into a corner.

Pushed by Adrian, maybe? I could see how that might happen. If Adrian wanted some get-rich-quick money, and if he thought Nana was a way to get his hands on some he'd rope Mum into helping him.

And if Mum truly thought Nana was sick, well, she might try to use that. So she'd be in favor of me going back to the river house to talk to Nana and explain how Mum needed to borrow money to invest in Adrian's scheme.

And if Nana really was sick, someone like Adrian might think it was a good time to push her to agree to what he wanted.

I wanted to get in first.

I phoned Nana from a telephone booth with the last of the credit on the phone card she'd given me. She sounded just like always, and we chatted while I tried to work out what to say.

In the end I just said, "Nana, Mum says—she says you might not be feeling too good."

Nana laughed, one of her deep rich chuckles that seemed to start down at her toes and stayed deep in her throat. It was comforting to hear but I wasn't completely convinced.

"You'd tell me if you weren't well, wouldn't you?" I persisted. There was a pause and then her voice came strong and firm.

"Yes, I would. I swear I would."

"So Mum's wrong?"

Another laugh. "Seems that way, doesn't it?"

"But why would Mum say you were sick if you're not?" I could think of reasons, but I wanted to know what Nana would say. There was another pause. I listened as hard as I could, because sometimes the bits where people don't say anything—when they're working out what to say—tell you more than words do.

"Jessye girl, your mother gets fancies and ideas of her own devising and the lord only knows where they come from. And after a time, she thinks they're true even if they're not. I can't tell you why she thinks it but I swear to you I'm fine. Missing you! But fine."

I thought, Maybe she doesn't even know that she's sick. I was still frightened of the swirl of dark water that had sucked me under, and the tentacle stayed wrapped around my heart, squeezing it with fear.

That's when I knew I had to go home to the river house and see her. I couldn't be sure about anything unless I asked her, face-to-face. And I wanted to ask her—warn her—about Mum and Adrian and the money, too. Not that Nana couldn't cope with them; she'd be okay with one hand tied behind her back is what she usually said about people trying to put one over her.

If I got away from Mum for a while I could think straight about her. I couldn't work out what to do anymore, but if I could just get back to the river and be quiet and peaceful for a while, I'd be able to think: about the story Lovey had told me; about my dead uncle; about the vanished houses on the river. About my disappeared father. And about the taniwha.

I woke up in the middle of the next night because someone came home late and slammed the front door. And when I was lying awake beside Mum I suddenly thought, I don't have to take up her ideas about what the dream meant. I could go with what my own head tells me about it.

It was like a light clicked on, and I knew something I hadn't known before. I suddenly thought, what if the taniwha was trying to tell me something? But not about Nana—about me.

What if the taniwha wants me, and it's sending me the dream, and the water? If it needs help to get out of the dark and lonely night where it's been so long, and I'm the one to do that?

You'd think that would be a most frightening thought to have, but once I'd had it, it wasn't. It was almost a relief.

It was easy to persuade Mum I should go back to Nana. Too easy in a way; I was hurt when she took it so well because usually she tried to talk me into staying. I've heard her on the phone to Nana often enough arguing to keep me for longer, saying she needed me to stay and do this or that with me. She'd say she had things planned for us even when she didn't; she'd make up some project in a flash and she'd even have me thinking she'd been planning it all along. Usually, she just didn't want to let me go.

This time it was different. She was still annoyed with me, which I was familiar with, although it didn't usually last. Mum's moods shifted around like island weather—bright one minute and stormy the next, then bright again before you'd registered the last patch of cloud. Now her weather seemed stuck on stormy. And it wasn't only that I wanted her to mind me going, and wanted her to miss me if I wouldn't be around for a while. It was more that I missed her being like she had always been in the past—holding on tight; getting me to stay.

It's funny how when she did that I used to feel confused and unhappy—and when now suddenly she didn't do it, I didn't like that, either. Nana would laugh at me if she knew. She'd say, *"There's no pleasing some people!"* But the trouble was clear as day to me now. I could almost see Mum's mind ticking over. Jessye can talk to her grandmother about the money—she might as well have said it out loud. And now I knew I'd been right about Adrian putting the money idea in her head, or anyway keeping it cooking away. I'd seen them together with their heads bent so close that Mum's curls were tickling his ear and I heard what Adrian was saying, because he's not a good whisperer. Some people, men especially, I've noticed they can't seem to lower their voices enough to whisper. I wasn't trying to hear, but I caught the words, anyway.

"Can't you get her to mention it? Sound her out for us? Wouldn't that work?"

I'd have to be dumber than dumb not to know what he meant.

And I'd have to be dumber than dumb to help either of them try to get any money out of Nana.

Chapter Nine

So I left early on Saturday morning with the half-finished plastic-bag chicken squashed into my backpack along with everything else. I worried about that all the way across Auckland to pick up the first long bus ride north, about how I was going to finish it without the art room tools. And then I started worrying how much it was my fault it hadn't worked with Mum this time.

I reckon Mum was sorry to see me go in the end. I knew I'd miss being with her, too, and at the last moment I wondered if I should change my mind and stay longer. But then Adrian came in, and right away Mum changed back to how she was when he was around, like I wasn't a priority for her. So I was relieved to be going.

Worrying about Mum lasted me all the way north to the town where I changed buses. And while I waited for the next one—the bus that would take me through to the ferry landing—I decided I'd done enough worrying. Either it was partly my fault about Mum, or it wasn't. If it was true, well, I couldn't do anything about it now. And if it wasn't true, I still couldn't do anything about it. Same with the chicken.

I felt relieved, like a weight had lifted off me, and I slept right through the last rocking, noisy bus journey. I didn't wake up again until it stopped and I was as squashed as the chicken was in my backpack, wedged against the edge of the seat and the side of the bus with a crick in my neck. I wondered for a moment why the bus had stopped and where I was, and then a waft of sea smell blew through the bus window and I knew I was at the harbor crossing and almost home again.

Home to the silvery sweep of the river, and the chunks of dark forest rising from the little sloping hills. My harbor of trees and tides.

I stood out on the deck as the ferry crossed the harbor. There was a cold wind and the water was dark; you couldn't see through it, not even in the shallow bits. I waited to see what would happen, if there'd be some sort of sign to help me work things out, but nothing did. And I thought again about the taniwha, how it hid its own secrets under the river, and how if you saw it at all it was only a flash in the corner of your vision, or a moment in a dream. There was a lot I was carrying around; a lot of knowledge that I didn't really want, and a lot of other people's secrets. I wondered how many of my own secrets I really understood. Maybe I didn't know as much as I thought; maybe all I had was the flash of the taniwha's tail, or the swish of a tentacle in the darkness of a dream.

I got a ride up from the ferry landing with Irma, who

runs our local shop. She took me all the way to Nana's corner and I balanced a box of pastries on my lap to keep them from tipping over. Irma chatted away about how the wholesaler always got her orders wrong, and how she'd told him often enough, and so on. I didn't have to reply and she didn't expect me to, she just wanted to sound off while I kept the pastries safe.

I knew Nana would have an eye out for me on the road, and an ear out as well for a car stopping, in case I'd got a ride. But when I turned the corner from the road and opened the gate, I didn't see her.

What I saw was the doctor's car, parked out in front.

I felt bewitched; I couldn't move or speak. I once read a story about a boy who turned to stone on the outside, although he was still a human being on the inside. It was like that. Every breath was suddenly an effort, but my brain was going full gallop. I was thinking things like, she lied! Nana lied to me! She really is sick, like Mum said. And then again, She lied to me! It was the lying that filled my mind at first: not what Nana being sick would mean, not right off.

But when I walked in, Dr. Gullick and Nana were sitting having a cup of tea and chatting on about recycling like any ordinary day. Maybe it was? Maybe I was wrong? I knew, though, as soon as I studied Nana's expression. She's never been that good at concealing her feelings and she hasn't got better at hiding them, plus I've got better at reading the signs. As soon as I arrived Nana knew what I'd be thinking, and she looked embarrassed, like she'd been caught out. As embarrassed as Tu, the time I found him up on the table. When he saw me he'd given a sort of squeak, like he was saying—*I know I'm not supposed to be up here!* Of course Nana didn't squeak, but her expression said the same thing: *I've been found out.* So I knew.

Dr. Gullick said she'd stay for that second cup of tea after all so she could hear what had been going on with me. So we chatted for a while, and got on to what had been going on in the district since I'd been gone. Recycling was still the prime issue, though. I should have whipped out my plastic-bag chicken: Dr. Gullick would love it. She's a recycling freak, never so happy as when she's squashing up cardboard boxes and nagging people about sorting their trash into different categories. I once saw her down at the dump in the pouring rain, singing away while she stacked up soggy bundles of old newspapers.

Neither of them talked about why the doctor was there. The doctor wasn't going to mention Nana's health to me without Nana's say-so, and Nana was trying to work out what to say to me once the doctor had gone. I was upset, and of course she knew that. How I felt now was making up for all the times when I hadn't got angry with her because I'd seen her point of view, and it looked better than mine did.

"I had no plans to lie to you, my little mokopuna, but I didn't have time to tell you the truth, either."

Nana paused, and then started again.

"When I was just a bit older than you, and at high school in the city, my mother got sick and I had to come back and look after her. Not that I minded, eh—I loved her, and I wanted to take care of her. But it was the end of my schooling."

She'd never told me that before. I wondered if she'd had plans to go on, do her exams, and maybe get some qualifications. And she said yes, she had done; she'd wanted to train as a nurse.

"I wanted to be a district nurse—you know, like the ones back in the old days traveling up and down the country taking care of people who lived so far from any hospital that medical help had to come to them? But my mother didn't get better, and after she died I stayed on at home; looked after my father, brought up my sisters. I never did get back into books and education."

"And you thought if you told me you were sick I'd come running back and miss out on the chance of city schooling?" I started to see what had happened.

"Got it in one, girl," Nana agreed with a wry smile. "Well? Wouldn't you?"

"But I'm here now, anyway," I pointed out. "And you knew I'd be back soon. So what's the difference? I'm not missing out, you know. I'll be back at Waimotu school on Monday, for the last weeks of the term."

"The difference is that you've got to start thinking about high school," Nana answered firmly. "That's where you'll be next year. And you have to choose where you'll be, and stick with it. You can't skip and jump around from school to school when you're working toward exams. That's the difference."

"Mum told me you were sick." I saw what Nana meant about high school, but I wanted to get back to her health. "And you said she was making it up, but it looks to me that she wasn't!"

Nana sighed, and gave a small smile.

"April *doesn't* know what's wrong," she pointed out. "She couldn't. The doctor doesn't know yet. I started to feel sick last week, but I didn't think anything of it then. Now it's got worse, so Dr. Gullick did a few tests, and she stopped by to talk about them. And I'll tell you straight, girl, it's only today that she said I'll have to go into the hospital."

Nana said she'd had a bit of stomach pain the week before, but she'd only talked to the doctor when it started to wake her up in the night. She said the pain came and went—"like the tides, Jessye," she claimed with a grin. "Mostly, it's nothing much. But even so, I reckoned I'd check with the doctor."

So *had* Mum been right, in a way? Maybe when she was here she'd sensed that Nana wasn't well, before Nana knew herself? Could that happen?

Nana got up to check the oven, where she had dinner started. I told her I'd do it, she only had to say what she wanted, and we argued comfortably until she let me take over the cooking under her instructions, and sat down again on the sofa with Tu on her lap. He didn't often get the chance.

"She rang, you know, last night," she said. I knew she meant Mum. She must have phoned while I was packing.

"April wanted to borrow some money," Nana went on.

"She said you'd tell me all about the project she needed it for." She looked at me thoughtfully, and then grinned. "What do you think I said?"

I was glad I hadn't had to bring up the subject, or admit straight out that Mum had gone off the rails again; she'd made it plain herself.

"Something about a fool and her money?" I suggested with a straight face. "A fool and his money are soon parted" was one of Joe's favorite sayings. Nana laughed.

"Close enough," she agreed.

I wondered if I should say I hadn't been going to talk about Mum's project. But Nana probably understood how things stood.

"And this Adrian fellow, he got mentioned a lot. He's the one you don't like too much, eh?" Nana asked.

I nodded, but then I put up my hand to contradict myself. "I liked him okay to start with, but I've gone off him big time. Mum thinks he's great, though; Adrian's top dog as far as she's concerned. She believes everything he says, but what he says doesn't sound that great to me. . . ." I trailed off because I didn't want to go into details, and I didn't want to mention the drinking. Nana didn't push it. I bet she'd worked it all out.

"So what did April say was wrong with me, anyway?" Nana asked, putting Tu gently aside, getting up from the sofa again and waving away my protests. I told her about Mum's leukemia theory.

"Well, she didn't pick the right bit of me to need sorting," she said calmly, settling down at the table with a bowl of beans from the garden. I'd brought her back a gadget to slice beans into long strips, like spaghetti. It gets rid of the stringy bits at the sides, too. We took turns to push the beans through it.

"Dr. Gullick says it could be a few different things causing the pain," Nana went on, when we had our bean production line worked out. "The blood tests didn't give a clear answer one way or another, so she's finding me a hospital bed so the doctors there can watch me, and work it out. Maybe as soon as next week—she says sooner's better. But you listen to me now, eh? She says there's no call for concern. You could talk to her if you like, get it straight in your head; ask whatever questions you need for your own peace of mind. It might stop you worrying about me, eh?"

I smiled weakly and passed the bean machine back to her. Nana smiled ruefully back.

"Yeah, okay, Jessye girl, that doesn't sound likely, eh? You'll worry, anyway, I know that. But I know what it's like when people won't give things a proper name. My mother got sicker and sicker, and no one would tell me what was wrong with her. Or they told me lies. It was cancer—breast cancer, Jessye, and a bad one—but no one wanted to say it out loud in those days."

She sighed, and put down the bowl of beans. "So I want you to know the whole truth about this; know how to confront it, outstare it face-to-face."

I thought about that.

"Like naming a taniwha?" I suggested.

Nana looked at me thoughtfully.

"What brought that up?"

I shrugged; I didn't want to mention my ideas about the taniwha to her yet.

"Naming a taniwha's a tricky business," she said, frowning. "You might not know its real name. Or the taniwha mightn't want you to say it out loud to the world."

"But if you do it, anyway . . ."

She looked at me again and finally nodded.

"If you do, then yes. Naming it will give you power— over yourself, maybe, not the taniwha. But power for sure, Jessye girl."

We talked back and forth, working out what I'd do when Nana was in the hospital. Nana didn't want to leave me by myself. She thought I should get someone in to stay with me, or I should stay with Joe. She even suggested I might go back and stay with Mum again, which had to be a first.

She didn't insist on her ideas, though, and I held out against staying somewhere else. I knew that Lovey was coming back to Waimotu soon, so maybe she could stay with me? And in the end Nana agreed that I could stay in the river house, "at least to start with," and the doctor and Joe would drive me in to see her in the hospital, and as soon as her pains were diagnosed, well, we'd take it from there.

"We'll see how you do by yourself, and with Lovey, eh? Anyway, I reckon I'll be home in no time. Those hospital doctors'll straighten me out."

"Wouldn't dare not to, eh?" I teased, sounding more cheerful than I felt.

The next week was a whirl. I was back at Waimotu school in the daytime, and getting Nana ready for the hospital in the evenings. We made time to try out the lemonade recipe she'd mentioned weeks back—it's easy, too, I can do it myself now. Nana phoned Mum to tell her what was happening; I phoned Lovey to check she was still coming down, which she was. Nana and I cooked up some meals for the freezer, and Joe took us into town for a big supermarket shop. Nana even let me organize that, although she kept a close eye on my choices. She's almost as keen on healthy eating as she is on recycling, but I still managed to nab packets of chocolate fish for me and Lovey.

Dr. Gullick picked Nana up the next Sunday to drive her to the hospital; they were starting a new round of tests first thing on Monday morning. Of course, we'd been through everything all over again just before she left.

"You'll be all right, Jessye, here by yourself until Lovey comes tomorrow? You're still okay with that? Joe'll look in on you, or you could still change your mind, go and stay with him if you like, but you'll be happier here, eh? You can call the hospital, maybe talk to me tonight if you like. Or if you'd rather—"

I'd stopped her there.

"Or if I'd rather—nothing! It'll be fine, Nana, honestly. I'll be fine. Don't worry about it. Just concentrate on getting better fast." I hugged her hard.

"It's legal to leave me on my own, you know," I teased her. "I'm old enough."

She took me seriously, though.

"I know that, child," she said, frowning for a moment as she hugged me back. "Or I wouldn't do it."

I could hear the doctor's car going up the hill, changing down through the gears to climb around the top corner. Then a sort of peacefulness wrapped itself around the afternoon like a scarf, and I sat on the steps and watched the wind pull silvery ribbons of water across the river. After all our running around, the silence seemed very loud, and the not-Nana space was big in my mind. I knew the hospital was the right place for her, though. I reckoned the pain had got worse during the week, although she hadn't said so.

I looked at Tu sleeping in the afternoon sunshine against the woodpile, and listened idly to the sounds ebbing and flowing around the end of the afternoon. Cars on the road up from the ferry; shouts and laughter from a fishing boat going out to catch the evening tide; a snatch of song from a truck down the road.

No, not from a truck—from the river. I got the field glasses to have a closer look. There was a group of men hauling a big canoe out of the water; a proper traditional one. One of the men was wearing a red jacket, and it stood out like a flaring match against the greens and silvers of the mangroves and the water.

Nana had told me there'd be a hui on the marae the next weekend; a meeting to discuss ideas for a bridge across the river. She was sorry to miss it; she has a lot to say about a bridge. As you'd expect. Anyway, this must be the new canoe for the opening ceremonies, and what I'd heard was the chant that went with getting it out of the water.

I couldn't hear the words clearly, so I looked it up in Nana's books and wrote down the one I think is right—I'll check it when they do the chant for real. This is what I reckon they said; it's a really old one:

Toia mai i te waka!
Ki te moenga,
Te waka!
Ki te takoto runga i takoto ai,
Te waka!

And that means:

Pull the canoe!
To the berth,
The canoe!
To the resting place to lie,
The canoe!

They were hauling it over the bank, and up past the mangroves to dry ground. It was quite a sight—Nana'll be sorry she missed that, too.

The phone rang an hour or so later, and it was Dr. Gullick to say that Nana was settled into her room in the hospital. "They'll start doing more tests tomorrow, and she's hooked up to machines to monitor her heart and blood pressure and I don't know what else," she said. "She told me the pain had gone again, but they'll get her straightened out, don't you worry."

"You reckon she'll be home soon, though?" I asked. Silly question, I know, but I asked it, anyway.

"Depends what the problem is, Jessye—so let's wait and see what they say tomorrow." And then she moved into a set of questions for me: Was I really okay? Wouldn't I like to spend the evening with her and her family? Maybe stay the night? I said again that I was fine, and I had my dinner on the stove, and Uncle Joe was dropping in later and he'd pick me up for school the next day. The dinner bit was true, although I was only heating fish pie. The Joe bit wasn't completely true but it could have been, I wasn't really telling a lie. I didn't know he *wouldn't* drop in that evening. And he *was* picking me up for school in the morning because he was going there, anyway, to do their office accounts.

The truth was, I wanted more time by myself.

So I sat on the front steps again, and thought about everything. About Nana lying in a strange hospital bed in the smart new pajamas we'd bought for her, and whether she'd be frightened. She'd not admitted to worrying about it, let alone being frightened, but I thought she must have been. Anyone would be. She was just used to putting on a brave face.

And I thought about Mum, which is easier to do when she isn't around. About how having Adrian in her life was so important to her, and how I wished I could make her see that he wasn't right for her. Then I had a rush of wishing that Mum wasn't . . . well, to be honest, I wished she wasn't like she is, which is softhearted to a fault. Mum'll even admit to herself that she's too softhearted, although she's brave as well. When things don't work out she doesn't give up, she always starts again. But I didn't want to watch Mum get hurt anymore.

The light faded slowly and everything lost its colors, like someone was rinsing them out while I watched. By the time I went back inside the wind had got up, and it smelled of rain. The river was as dark as night; almost black, with a rough kind of spikiness moving across the surface like the edge of a serrated knife.

The wind grew stronger while I ate, but I didn't realize how much until I opened the back door and a gust slammed me in the chest as hard as a fist. Tu rushed past me into the house with his fur all fluffed up. He didn't often spend the night inside and I wondered if he knew we were in for a storm. I turned on the radio for news, but the crackle was so bad I couldn't hear the program. Still, I knew someone would phone or come by if anything serious was on the way, so I pushed storm worries to the back of my mind along with my worries about everything else. I reckon you can only do so much worrying about any one thing at any one time. Or maybe you should rotate worries, like crops in the garden?

I gave the recycled chicken another try. Tu was fascinated by the rustling of the plastic and he started pouncing and patting it with his paw, just like a playful kitten. He never did that when Nana was around. But I'd only just started fiddling with the feathery bits when there was a crash outside. It had a clang inside it, and it was probably the washhouse door. I'd got as far as thinking should I try to fix it before everything inside the shed got soaked, and wondering whether doing that in the stormy dark was all that good an idea, when there was a loud knock at the door. A moment later, Lovey burst through it.

She was soaking wet, head to foot, like she'd had a shower with all her clothes on. She stood on the mat dripping and laughing, and then she whirled her hair around her head, like when a dog comes out of the sea and shakes itself dry. Drops of water flew everywhere, and Tu dived under the sofa.

Then the lights went out.

For a moment neither of us said anything, and then Lovey laughed again.

"Great entrance, eh?" she said. "Better than any play. Better than a horror film, even."

"It couldn't be a play," I pointed out, standing still and waiting for my eyes to adjust to the dark. "The stage would be pitch-black, which would ruin the whole effect. A movie would be better; you could light the set so that the only thing you saw"—I paused while I fumbled around on a shelf for the flashlight, and found it—"was someone's face."

And I caught Lovey's face in the beam of light.

"Talking about entrances . . ." I added, and raised my eyebrows at her.

"What am I doing here tonight?" Lovey supplied. I handed her the kitchen towel so she could start drying off, and felt around the kitchen drawers for candles and matches.

"Rangimarie's come up to see her mother," she said, her voice muffled by the towel around her head. Rangimarie was her mother's sister with a job in a law office in town, but she came home to Waimotu whenever she could. Lovey rubbed hard and then shook her head, and her hair whirled around again with less splashing.

"So I thought I'd get a ride with her for free, come a day early and see how you're doing," she added. "She dropped me off at the corner, which now I think about it was dumb, because you might not have been in. Then I'd have had to get back down the road and up the hill in the dark and the rain."

I hung the wet towel over the rail on the stove.

"So your nana's gone in?" she asked, glancing around. "You were going to be by yourself tonight if I didn't come?"

"Nah, the cat's looking after me," I teased. "Lovey, honestly, I'm fine. You sound like a nana yourself, worrying about things."

"So, anyway," she said, and fell silent again, which was unusual for Lovey. I looked at her expectantly but she didn't finish her sentence because there was a splintering flicker of lightning and a loud crash of thunder. I counted the seconds between them: less than before. The heart of the storm was moving our way.

My first thought was how lucky it was that Nana was in the hospital, because she hates storms. The hospital was on the other side of the mountain so they weren't likely to have the same weather—you could leave Waimotu in peaceful sunshine and drive over the mountain into a hail-storm. And vice versa.

And my second thought was that I should try to fix the door. It was probably crazy to go outside but suddenly that was the only thing I wanted to do. Wild weather can take hold of you in strange ways. I couldn't say exactly what inspired me.

"I'm going outside!" I shouted to Lovey over the crash of more thunder and the loud thrum of rain on the roof. "The shed!" I added, waving my hand toward the side of the house. Lovey looked at me in alarm. She'd just had a go at getting dry and she can't have wanted to go out again. Still, she was up for it.

I felt my way to the back door and braced myself to open it.

Then a whole lot of things happened, one after the other. Like when you're building a house out of playing cards, which I have tried to do, one careful card at a time, and it's all fine until you add one too many. You don't know which card that's going to be; it's only after you put it in place you can tell. Then the whole thing wobbles a little and then it wobbles more, and, for a moment, you hope it'll be okay. First one card moves and others follow—and then the whole pack slides. And everything falls down.

Chapter Ten

If you've ever been out in a storm you'll know how it can be a mixture of exhilarating and frightening, and it was all of that as soon as we stepped outside. Lovey knew what to expect, but I didn't. I'd heard the wind and rain from inside the house, but the full force of it was another world. The wind's shriek slapped into your ears, and the trees groaned as they twisted around, all in the pitch dark and the pelting rain. I was soaked through in a minute, and Lovey's drying off was wasted.

We did try to fix the washhouse door, which was flapping like a sheet on the washing line, but all we could do was jam it shut with logs and hope they'd hold. When we turned back for the house, my eye was caught by something down on the road. Something was there that shouldn't be. I looked again, narrowing my eyes against the rain and dark and standing as still as the wind would allow, trying to understand what wasn't right.

The next slivers of lightning lit up the answer. The water was up over the road! I'd caught its glint in a patch of light but my eyes hadn't recognized it until I stopped and stared. I grabbed Lovey's shoulder to turn her around, and pointed.

"Was it like that when you got here?" I shouted in her ear, and she followed my pointing finger with her eyes.

"No!" she shouted back, and then started to laugh. I could see why. She couldn't have got through if the road had been flooded; no one could, the water was too high.

Lovey's laughter swept me into the excitement of the storm. We started to leap about like crazy people, whirling around, slipping and sliding in the mud, and yelling with laughter. The rain ran into our eyes and dripped off our noses, and ran into our mouths as soon as we opened them. I started singing, and Lovey whirled around with her long hair swinging like wet rope. Then she turned and shouted something straight into the storm. It would have sent shivers up my spine if I'd been dry enough for shivers, because what she shouted was from my dream. It was what the tentacle had said:

"To Po nui!
Te Po roa!
Te Po kerekere!"

I peered at the river and the road again, and I could see the water lapping farther across the land, swallowing it up. The long night of deep shadows is what it was, all right. And I knew what I had to do.

I had to talk to the taniwha.

I felt heavy with fear, but even so I was sure about

doing it. I took a slippery step toward the water, and a deep breath to calm myself. And then Lovey was beside me in the dark and took my hand, which gave me courage, and I shouted out what was in my heart:

> *"I know your name!*
> *Your name is—The Captor of Hemi!*
> *Help me! Please help me!*
> *Nana's in the hospital!*
> *Dad's gone away!*
> *Don't flood the land again!*
> *We are your people, and I call on you—*
> *Please help me."*

And then I thought, should I have done that in Maori? Did taniwha understand English? I tried to remember how you do a formal good-bye in Maori. In ordinary situations it'd just be kia ora or haere mai, but talking to a taniwha's not that ordinary. And when I shouted it into the storm Lovey joined in, too, like she'd known what I was planning.

> *"Tena koe! Tena koe!"*

We stood there shivering for a bit after that but nothing actually happened—like, the taniwha didn't stick its nose out of the water. The storm didn't ease and the water didn't stop rising—not then, anyway. But something happened to me.

I felt different.

I felt more myself than I'd ever been before, is the only way I can explain it. Like, if you take ordinary days as being 100 percent yourself, then that night I was a 150 percent myself. More exciting, and more real than I could keep up for very long. But also more wonderful than I'd ever imagined feeling. And if that doesn't make any sense I can't help it: It's the best I can do in words.

If you've ever wanted to do something but you're too frightened to, and people say, *Go on! It'll be fine!* And you summon all your courage and dive in; do a bungee jump; whatever—and it's okay. You felt the fear but you did it, anyway, and then you're free from that fear forever.

I felt a bit like that.

Then Lovey and I went a bit mad, all over again. I was filled with excitement and power and daring and I danced around shouting every water word I could think of, and Lovey joined in.

"Waiwai!" I started it off. If you repeat a word it's like increasing its power—wai is water, so waiwai is lots of water.

"Hukanui!" called Lovey, which, she told me later, is the word for foaming water. The river was certainly doing that.

"How about the word for storm?" I shouted in her ear. Lovey laughed.

"I don't know the Maori word!" she said, pitching her tone to carry over the claps of thunder. "What about we call this a weather bomb and be done with it?"

I learned a load of words that night: whatitiri for the thunder and uira for the lightning. Ua, for rain, and hau for the wind, I knew already. We kept it up even when we were finally back inside the house, stoking up the fire and drying off again, with the rain still pounding on the roof.

"Dry is maroke," said Lovey, her voice muffled by the towel she had wrapped around her whole head. "Which will be nice."

I remembered the word for warm. "So will mahana, when we are," I told her.

"Do you reckon the river will go down again?"

"Not until the rain stops, anyway," Lovey decided.

"We probably shouldn't have gone outside when there was lightning," I remembered. "You can get struck by lightning in a storm. But Lovey—why did you say that bit from the creation story? That particular bit?"

Lovey paused, staring at me curiously.

"What bit?"

I reminded her.

"When?"

I was getting impatient. "When we were down at the river. Just now."

Lovey looked confused.

"I have no idea," she said. "I don't even remember saying it." She pulled an old sweater of Nana's over her head, and came out of it frowning.

"Did I really? It must have just come to me. The power of the moment?"

The power of the taniwha, more likely, is what I thought but didn't say.

The electricity stayed off all night, and it was still off when we woke early the next morning. The storm had eased back, but the air was heavy with mist under thick clouds. I thought it would rain again soon.

"Good thing Nana still likes to keep the wood oven working," I pointed out, when Lovey unrolled herself from the spare blankets on the sofa. "Or we couldn't have a hot breakfast."

We were eating toast and honey when Joe came over the back hill. We could hear him coming before we saw him; the mist muffled the sight of him but not the sound of his singing. He'd got through almost the whole of "Shenandoah" by the time he reached the veranda, and took off his muddy wet coat and boots.

That's such a great song. My favorite bit is this:

Oh Shenandoah, I love your daughter
Away you rolling river,
Though she won't cross your shining water
Away, I'm bound away,
Cross the wide Missouri.

Joe said he'd had breakfast but he'd be happy to eat another one, and what a night, eh? He stood warming himself up by the stove while I made more toast and topped up the hot water for his tea.

"Good to see you didn't flood or drown," he said. "I heard Lovey'd arrived so I wasn't worried when the phone lines went down. I couldn't get through on the river road, either, but I knew you two would be sensible; look after each other."

"How did you know Lovey was here?"

Joe grinned at me. "You've been away too long, girl." He was right; I'd forgotten how news moves around a place like Waimotu, even in a storm.

"The school's closed today, maybe longer," he added. "They got flooded. So Dr. Gullick says, would you like to drive to the hospital with her this afternoon, check on your nana? Dr. Gullick can't use this road, but she'll pick you up at the top corner about two."

Lovey and I spent the morning sorting things out in case the power outage continued. We found a stock of candles and filled up the oil lamps, and got in more wood for the stove. I was worried about the food in the freezer, but Lovey pointed out that the best thing to do was nothing. If you didn't open the door, the food had a better chance to stay cold.

"We should eat up the things in the fridge, though," I said. "And drink them, for that matter. Did you see the lemonade?" I'd made three big bottles of it. I looked at them proudly, and decided I'd take one in to Nana.

By lunchtime the mist had lifted. The river road was still thick with gluey mud, but you could walk through in rubber boots if you were careful. After lunch Lovey borrowed a spare pair and picked her way off to see that

Rangimarie's family were okay, and I went with her as far as the top of the hill, to wait for Dr. Gullick to pick me up.

"Don't let Mina worry about the river rising," was Joe's parting shot. "She'll only think back to the last time and get upset." Joe had never mentioned the last flood to me before. I expect the weather was making him think of Hemi.

Dr. Gullick warned me on the journey—even Joe had given me a hint about how it would be—but the sight of Nana in the hospital shocked me. She looked so small in the bed, and she's not small. She was like a different person; almost as though she was the child and I was the grown-up. I'd never thought of her being anything other than just Nana, who did everything for everyone and was a rock in my life. The rock at the center of it.

Her face was drawn, and she admitted the stomach pains were worse. "So this is the right place to be, eh?" she said. The hospital was still doing tests on her. Even in the short time I was there, a nurse came along and stuck a thermometer in Nana's mouth. She said it had to stay there for three minutes and no talking meanwhile, Mrs. Cooper.

Nana was trying so hard to reassure me, and I wanted to reassure her right back. I remembered an old gold-rush song that she sang to me when I was little; it goes to the tune of a nursery rhyme so it's not hard to sing. The chorus goes like this:

Gold, gold, gold
Bright fine gold

125

Wangapeka, Tuapeka
Gold, gold, gold.

The Maori words are the names of gold-rush towns in the South Island, but now the song just made me think of Mum and Adrian, and the money they wanted from Nana.

I had a glass of lemonade ready for her when the thermometer came out again, and a joke about her losing weight because they hadn't let her eat anything. I told her how Lovey had arrived, and how the power and the phone were still off, so I'd rely on Dr. Gullick to get hospital news on her cell phone and pass it on. I told her about the school closing, and even heard myself saying that I'd keep up my schoolwork at home. Then a nurse came back to do more things just when Dr. Gullick turned up, so we had to go.

When I kissed Nana good-bye she didn't even smell right. She smelled of hospitals and disinfectant.

We drove back over the mountain into a stormy sky and a splatter of rain. I got Dr. Gullick to drop me at Rangimarie's house, because I knew Lovey would still be there. They're on high ground so they hadn't flooded; they hadn't even lost their electricity. They said ours would be on again now, the electricity guys had fixed the Waimotu supply, but the school would probably be closed all week.

"You'll be back at your desk next week, I bet, and no more slacking off," Rangimarie's friend teased me. "Lovey, too, if she stays on."

"That's the last week of the term, though," Lovey pointed out with a triumphant smile. "You can always slack off in the last week!" I didn't tell Lovey what I'd promised Nana, about carrying on with schoolwork, anyway, but I was determined: a promise is a promise.

We left Rangimarie's house loaded with food. We wouldn't have to cook anything that night; just heat up what we'd been given. We got back to the river house safely, although we had to concentrate hard on balancing everything without slipping in the mud, so I didn't notice anything different. And when the front door suddenly opened and Mum and Adrian were standing in the doorway, well, my jaw must have dropped open in astonishment.

I'd phoned Mum the week before about Nana going into the hospital, and I'd expected her to say, *Come back up here then, Jayjay, and we'll have fun!* And I guessed she might say something like, *I told you so!* about Nana being sick. But she hadn't said any of that, only, *Was I all right?* So I thought I'd just wait for her to stop sulking and be her normal self again, which is what always happened in the end. I hadn't expected her to come around literally—or so quickly.

Mum and Adrian were full of how difficult their journey down had been, and how they'd been told they wouldn't be able to get through because of the storm, and how the ferry wouldn't be running—although when they got to the harbor, "*Of course* it was running!" said Mum triumphantly. "And we walked up from the ferry landing because no one's driving on this sloppy road, the water's still too high. We had to pick our way around the edge of the really gooey bits, and cut across fields, and everything! I couldn't call because the phones were down, so I couldn't even say we were coming, or when we'd arrive. But you like surprises, don't you, Jayjay? And this is a good one, isn't it?"

I smiled and gave her a hug. I was pleased to see her but I couldn't tell if it was a good surprise or a bad one. Not yet.

Lovey had met Mum several times, but she hadn't met Adrian. I was curious to know what she'd think—I'd told her a bit about him. He was in one of his let's-be-charming-to-everyone moods and he sprang up to help Lovey get a meal ready for us all, and bustled outside for more logs even though we didn't need them—with the power back on. I had to admit he was showing willingness.

Mum and I sat on the front veranda for a chat, while Lovey and Adrian got the food ready. I explained about going to see Nana, and how they were still doing tests, trying to work out what was wrong.

"Dr. Gullick's going to keep in touch with the hospital on her cell phone," I added. "Then she'll let me know some way or other as soon as they know; take me back in tomorrow if she can."

Mum nodded. "I reckon I'll come with you next time." It was a statement, not an inquiry. There'd be room in the car, no question about that, but I didn't think Mum coming to the hospital was a good idea, not if she might say something to upset Nana. But I didn't know how to bring that up, so I left it. Mum might change her mind. Or she'd have to figure it out with Dr. Gullick.

"Why have you two come down now?" I asked straight out. "Not for the hui, I bet." I didn't think Mum cared if we had a bridge or not.

Mum grinned at me. She was full of bounce and cheerful with it.

"Not the hui, no. But I decided to sit down with Mina and talk about the money. And no, Jayjay, there's no need for you to make that face," she added as I looked at her in disbelief. "Let me finish. I only want to explain the project to her properly, so she understands why I need her to invest in it. Once she understands that; sees what a good idea it is, well then—"

I couldn't believe what I was hearing.

"You are NOT planning to hassle Nana about this NOW?" I heard my voice rising and I didn't care. "You couldn't be so . . . so . . ."

I couldn't find the right words. Mum had the grace to blush, but being embarrassed didn't stop her.

"Listen to me, Jayjay," she said, her voice dropping. "I've found out something else, something important. About you, in fact. And that's really going to help a lot."

"Help what?" I didn't get it.

"Help me—well, help us all actually, darling. It's about the land. I went to talk to the people at the Maori Land Office, and they said it was all down to you!"

I stared at her with my mind racing and all the old fears and worries rushing into my mind. I couldn't think what she meant, let alone did I even want to know, but then Lovey flung open the door behind us, and shouted, "Kai's on the tepu!" with a wicked grin at me.

Lots of people mix Maori words into English sentences and lots of people say "kai" for food, too. But when Lovey and I had spouted Maori water words at each other the night before it was just a game, not how you'd do it in ordinary life. And the way Lovey did it now, adding "tepu" for table like that? Well, even without her grin, I guessed that Lovey was ridiculing someone, and Adrian was the obvious candidate. I wondered what he'd done to annoy her.

"Oh, that's so interesting!" Adrian said, popping out on to the veranda behind Lovey. He was overdoing it, all bright eyes and bushy tail. I figured he was nervous, and I suddenly wondered if he'd ever been in such a Maori part of the country before—coming over on the ferry with people arriving for the hui, then Nana's house, then Lovey teasing him. He probably felt in over his head.

"I think that must be what's called Maori English!" he went on, smiling widely at Lovey.

"Not really," she answered with a straight face, deliberately misunderstanding him. "Down here we call it teatime."

Adrian's smile froze for a moment, but then he recovered bravely.

"Down here?" he asked, frowning. "You can't mean down by the river? Because I thought we were up—up is north, so why do you say it's down?"

Even Mum grinned, and she took pity on him as we went back inside. "It is up on a compass, Adrian, but it's down to the tail of Maui's fish. That's the North Island—it's the fish that Maui caught, in the old story. The fish's head is Wellington, and the tail fin's at the other end, where we are now."

"Te ika a Maui," I went on. "It means 'the fish of Maui.' The South Island's his waka—his canoe."

"Up is down," added Lovey helpfully, her eyes still sparkling as she carried an extra chair to the table. I giggled; I couldn't help it. Adrian shot a suspicious look at me but I managed to smooth out my face, so he couldn't be sure he was being mocked.

Dr. Gullick phoned before we'd finished eating—I didn't even know the phone was on again until it rang.

"Sorry to disturb you, Jessye," she said, her voice coming through a worse-than-usual crackle. "I'm back at the hospital. Your grandmother's not doing quite as well as we'd like, but at least we know what's wrong with her now."

My stomach lurched. Her voice was tinny in my ear and the static made it hard to hear, and I struggled to follow what she was saying.

"It's appendicitis, Jessye. Not what you'd expect with someone her age, that's what slowed us down. But the doctors are sure; they're prepping her for surgery right now. Nothing to worry about, dear—and now we know we'll whip it out, and she'll be right as rain."

I smiled weakly at that. Rain wasn't always right—why did people say that, anyway? But Dr. Gullick's voice went on in my ear.

"She'll come around from the operation tonight and

will feel better tomorrow. Still, I'm not sure you should visit for a day or two, dear. It'll be visitors one at a time for a while, if that. It might be better to wait awhile . . ."

"They can't stop me going in, Dr. Gullick, can they? Not if you say it's okay? I really want to go." I was very certain no one could stop me seeing Nana—especially now. She'd need me. I knew she'd want me there, just like I'd want her if I was sick in a hospital.

Out of the corner of my eye I saw Mum swinging around to look at me but I didn't let her take the phone, and in the end Dr. Gullick agreed we should stick to tomorrow's visit. "No one else, mind," she said. "No friends or hangers-on, Jessye, not in her room, anyway."

So that dealt with the Mum question. She couldn't visit Nana. Even if she wouldn't take my no on board, she wouldn't get past the doctors or the hospital.

Chapter Eleven

Mum was on me as soon as I put the phone down, gabbing away nineteen to the dozen and hitting me with so many questions I couldn't answer one before she jumped to the next in line. So I sat her down again and explained what I knew about Nana's appendix operation, which wasn't much, while Lovey tried but failed to distract Adrian from joining in the conversation.

Later on I asked Lovey what she thought of him.

"I reckon he likes to cut a bit of a dash and be the big dog, but there's nothing much underneath except for *me! me! me!*" she said. "And that's the kind who get mean when things don't go their way." She's got a nose for stuff like that.

Mum was mad that she couldn't go and see Nana in the hospital; that's what she'd come up to do, she said. She went a bit sulky again when I explained what the doctor had said, and even sulkier when I stayed firm. But when we'd got over that I could see Mum was dying to talk to me about something else, but she didn't want to in front of Lovey. There was a bit of a mime act between her and

Adrian, all meaningful looks out of the side of their eyes, and gesturing with their heads, the way people do when they're trying to be subtle. In the end Adrian got to his feet and said in a false hearty tone, "Well, Lovey, what about it?"

Lovey and I looked at each other and then back at Adrian.

"Um, what about what?" I asked. Lovey just sat there looking comfortable.

Adrian produced his most winning smile.

"I hoped that Lovey would show me around," he said warmly. "Introduce me to that marae; I'd love to poke around a place like that and get the hang of it, especially with an expert guide on hand!"

There was a bit of a silence. Even Mum looked embarrassed. I didn't know where to start explaining what was wrong with almost every single word he'd said. Did he think a marae was some kind of theme park? Or an entertainment for casual passersby?

Marae aren't like that. There are rules about entering them, never mind walking around. Some parts are sacred and you have to treat them with proper respect. Nana says our marae is a taonga, which means a treasure, but it also means that it's a precious thing in our care. Sure, it's a collection of buildings, but it's the heart and soul of our community, too. We have certain ways to do things that don't include having people poke around. Visitors are greeted and welcomed but it's done properly, not just any old way.

You could say that it wasn't Adrian's fault he didn't know any of that, but when Mum tried to explain what was wrong he just got huffy. So she looked relieved when Lovey finally got to her feet.

"The thing is, I can't do that now, anyway," she said smoothly. "I promised to help prep food for the hui. Rangimarie's expecting me."

Sorry, she mouthed silently to me behind their backs as she picked up her jacket, and shrugged elaborately—meaning something like, *Yeah, but what can I do?*

"See you later," I said firmly and loudly on the *later*. I didn't want to be left alone with Mum and Adrian for too long. Whatever Mum wanted to talk about, I didn't expect I'd like it.

Once Lovey had gone I could see Mum casting around for something to occupy Adrian out of the house.

"Do we have enough wood for the stove?" she asked me innocently, although anyone could see she was really directing the question at Adrian to suggest—*Why don't you go outside and chop some more logs?*

I had a better idea.

"We've got lots of wood, but what about Nana's veggie garden?" I remembered how interested Adrian had seemed when I'd first told him about it.

"What a good idea, Jayjay! Isn't that a good idea, Adrian? You haven't done much gardening lately and you always used to say how much you liked it. You could give Mina a hand with hers, while she's in the hospital."

"The leek bed needs digging over," I added helpfully.

Adrian cast a suspicious look at me and then looked out the window.

"In the rain?" He sounded pretty unenthusiastic. It was raining again but not heavily enough to stop anyone; not in a place that gets as much rain as Waimotu. And Mum wasn't put off. So he grumbled his way into his parka, and sighed his way out onto the veranda to put on his boots.

"Thanks, sweetie!" Mum called after him. She turned back to me, her eyes shining with excitement. She leaned forward and patted my hand, like a conspirator.

"Now!" she said. "I can tell you!"

"Mum—" I suddenly dreaded hearing whatever she was going to say. For one awful moment I thought, She's going to tell me she wants to marry him!

"Here's the thing, Jayjay," she went on, her words tumbling out in excitement. "You know how we wanted to borrow money from Mina to set up a little business with the mineral drink? Or get her to invest in it herself?" I nodded cautiously.

"Well, Mina said she'd think about it when I phoned her, but I didn't reckon she meant it. She's too old-fashioned, you know that; she doesn't know a sound business opportunity when she sees one."

I started to interrupt but Mum plowed on.

"No, wait—hear me out on this. It was Adrian's suggestion that I should find out more about the land—and there's nothing wrong with doing that, don't look so disapproving."

Mum had found out about Nana's land? What on earth was going on? I stared at her unbelievingly.

"Just to clarify what the situation really was, and if the

land belonged to Mina outright or if she shared it with other people," Mum went on. "Adrian told me about the Maori Land Court, I didn't even know there was one—"

And then Mum paused dramatically, sort of interrupting herself. "Anyway, I found the answer. Mina's put it all in a special land trust. For you!"

There was a moment's silence. I could hear the rain getting louder on the roof and the muffled clang of the shed door out the back, which I thought must be Adrian getting garden tools. I didn't want to think about what Mum was saying. My mind was frozen.

"So it's *your* land now, Jayjay. Yours, and not your grandmother's after all."

Mum leaned forward across the table again, smiling in delight.

"So *you* can lend us the money if Mina won't come through! Isn't that terrific? You *will* lend it to us, won't you, darling? For my sake?"

"It's really pouring again," said Adrian, bursting in the back door at that exact moment. "I can't do any digging until it eases off." He unlaced his boots, put them by the stove, and then looked over at Mum and me, registering the uncomfortable silence in the room. He raised his eyebrows in mock surprise.

"Oh, sorry," he added sarcastically. "Did I interrupt something?"

I really lost it then.

"I do NOT believe this!" I knew I was shouting but I didn't care, not even when Mum sort of flinched back, her face full of surprise and alarm. She didn't get it. I loved her, no question, but I hated what she was doing. And now I knew that Adrian was the sleazeball I'd suspected. I just let it rip.

"How CAN you, Mum! How can you even THINK that I would help you trick Nana? That I'd go behind her back? Not when she's well and back on her feet, and never—NEVER—while she's lying in a hospital bed and can't even stop you. Well never mind. I can stop you!"

I was still shouting, right into Mum's face by now while Mum just stared at me, and Adrian stood with his face frozen in a mask of surprise.

"And, anyway, I don't believe it! I don't believe I really own Nana's land! But just supposing I did, then I wouldn't do anything to mess that up. Can't you understand that? If she's put it in a trust for me, well then she *trusts* me with it, doesn't she? Trusts me to keep it safe, trusts me not use it to help you lose money in another stupid scheme! Just because Adrian says you should!"

There was a sudden silence. I stared at Mum, willing her to understand what I was saying. But it was Adrian who answered me.

"You really shouldn't talk to your mother like that, Jessye," he said smoothly. His voice was low but the tone sent a shiver down my spine.

"This is between me and Mum," I said shakily. "Nothing to do with you."

I waited for Mum to agree, at least with that much, but she didn't say anything at all. Adrian did, though.

"And that's where you're wrong again," he said in the same soft tone. He walked across and stared at me with cold, snaky eyes. "Apologize to your mother now," he said with his hand on her shoulder.

"I'm sorry I was rude to you, Mum," I said carefully. "But I'm not sorry about what I said. I told the truth."

"If it's truth you want, then I'll give you some more of it," said Adrian in a conversational tone. Mum glanced up at him as if to interrupt but then she didn't say anything after all, and she didn't even look at me. She just put her hand on top of his, and looked down at the table again.

"You are a minor," said Adrian smoothly. "You're not 'of age' so you don't have the legal right to make your own decisions about anything, your parents do that for you until you're an adult. So right now you have to do what your mother says. She can get a court order, you know, she could even make you a ward of court if you're trouble-some. And if she wants to benefit from your land, well then, she can. You can't stop her."

Adrian paused for a moment, staring at me with this new, cold expression on his face. Like he was calculating how far he could push me. Then he shrugged.

"Like they say—deal with it, Jessye."

I couldn't believe what I was hearing. Mum couldn't possibly—she *wouldn't* agree with this! She just *couldn't*! I looked back at her in desperation. She was sitting at the table patting Adrian's hand that was resting on her shoul-der, and still not looking at me.

It couldn't be true.

I suddenly realized it sounded like a novel—an old-fashioned novel, set way back in Victorian times. Like the gold-rush song I'd sung to Nana. No one could *really* make me do what Adrian was saying. No one could make me betray Nana's faith in me.

If I could just hang on to that . . .

I looked straight at Adrian.

"You're a liar and a cheat and a fraud," I said. My voice came out as calm as his, although my stomach was churning with anger and fright. "And I don't know what you've done to Mum, why she won't stand up to you, but don't think you can bully me as well. You're not having it! Whatever you want from me, you're not having it! Try dealing with that, big dog!"

Then I turned and ran for the door.

I wished I'd grabbed my jacket because it was raining hard, but it was too late to go back for it. Adrian might try to stop me, even run after me, and I didn't want to hang about. I heard Mum shout, "Jayjay! Stop!" from inside the house but I jumped down through the railings onto the grass and ran, slipping in the mud but luckily not falling over, down to the gate.

My first idea was to find Lovey and tell her what had happened. Someone at Rangimarie's house might know what Adrian had been talking about, the Land Court stuff, and give me some advice. On the other hand, I didn't know them all that well, and this was sort of private . . .

Joe would know. He'd know about the money for sure,

and probably about the land, too. So instead of going down to the corner and then up the hill to look for Lovey, I cut along the riverbank. It wouldn't take me long to get to Joe's boundary line and then up to his house.

I concentrated so hard on pushing through the scrub along the bank without getting soaked, and not getting caught in the tall grass, that I didn't hear Adrian coming up behind me. I didn't even know he was there until he grabbed my shoulder and pulled me around.

"You—you little bitch! You're not getting away with this!"

I screamed and twisted away from him, and I broke his grasp but then I slipped over in the mud. Adrian sort of dived at me and got my leg, and we rolled around struggling. We were both soaked and covered in mud, which might have been funny if I hadn't been so frightened.

He sat up, still holding on to me, and shook the rain out of his eyes, but he didn't let go.

"Ow! That hurts!" It did, too.

"Like I said, little girl, *deal with it*," Adrian said through gritted teeth.

"What is your *problem*? What is this all about?"

Adrian stared at me, and then he threw back his head into the rain and laughed. It wasn't a friendly sound.

"You don't know anything, do you? Okay, I'll explain in simple words, little girl. Your mother and I, we need some money. And it seems that you have some. Is that clear enough?"

"You don't *need* some money at all!" I shouted. "You

could get some if you got a job—and Mum could, too, if you let her enjoy her job at Material World." I tugged against his hand, but he held on.

"And even if you did need money, you can't have mine, which I don't have, anyway!"

Adrian tightened his grasp.

"April and I, we have plans. We're going to make something of ourselves. She knows—she understands . . ."

I suddenly got it.

"You've told her you'll stay if she gets my money! That's it, isn't it? She thinks you won't stay with her unless you get it. Like some kind of bribe!"

Adrian just stared at me. He finally let go of me and stood up. I pulled myself up, too, rubbing my leg gingerly.

"That's disgusting!" I yelled at him. "That's the absolute pits! Mum really likes you; how can you be so mean? How can you use how she feels about you—use it against her?"

Adrian laughed again, but I'd had enough.

"Deal with THIS, why don't you!" I shouted, and slammed both my hands hard into his chest. He saw it coming but I hit him harder than I thought I could, and harder than he'd expected. And he slipped, and stumbled in the wet grass, and half got up, and then slipped again.

And while I watched in a sort of slow-motion dream, the clump of grass he was holding gave way—and he quietly slid into the river.

And then he disappeared under the water.

Chapter Twelve

What I first thought was, Of course he can swim. All New Zealanders learn to swim at school, even people who live in towns and don't have the sea or a river to swim in. So I wasn't worried about him drowning, I was just delighted he'd fallen in. That'll teach him, I thought.

I didn't want to stick around for when he crawled out, though, because he'd probably be in an even worse mood, and the man wasn't nice to start with. Mum shouldn't have anything to do with him.

I peered at the river to see if he'd started to swim back to the bank. The rain had eased but the river was still high—a lot higher than usual because of the flooding, even though the tide was going out.

And he wasn't there. The surface of the river was empty. There wasn't even a head showing above the water.

He'd gone under. Had he ever come up again? Maybe the current had caught him and he was being swept downstream? Maybe he'd hit his head when he went in?

Maybe he couldn't swim after all?

I hated and I despised him, but I couldn't let him drown.

I screwed up my eyes for another look, and then I heard someone behind me. My heart jumped and I whirled around in a panic—but it was Joe, running along the bank toward me with a coat on and another one draped over his head. I've never been so pleased to see anyone in my whole life.

"Heard some shouting," Joe called when he got closer. "You all right, girl?"

I was so relieved to see him that I burst into tears, which normally I would never do.

"It's Adrian," I sobbed, sliding back down to the ground. "I pushed him and he's fallen in the river, and the taniwha'll get him, or he'll drown. I think he might have drowned already." I had a terrible feeling now.

Joe didn't ask any more questions, which was a blessing, he just ran to the edge of the river and peered around.

"Can't see anything," he called. "He might have been swept on down!" He ran back and pulled me up, and wrapped the spare coat around me. Then he gave me a quick hug, and a little shake.

"Come on, girl, no time for this now, we have to sound the pahu, get everyone out!"

A pahu's a gong, although we don't actually have one of those. In the old days you sounded the pahu if the marae was attacked. What we have isn't even a bell, although it used to be one. Now it's an electronic alarm. When it sounds you can hear it absolutely everywhere, right down as far as the ferry landing.

It's really for the ambulance crew. If there's an accident on the top road the alarm rings, and the team on duty come running and drive the ambulance off to get people to the hospital. But you can use it for a local emergency as well, and everyone comes down to the ambulance shed to find out what's wrong.

I'd never been around to see how you switch it on. It's inside the shed and you have to know where the key is, which Joe did, of course. And then you set it to a continuous sound, instead of the *beep! beep! beep!* that calls the ambulance crew. Once it was going Joe went back to the river to keep looking for Adrian, and I stayed to tell people where to go.

Just about everyone in Waimotu turned out. Most people came on foot because the roads were still so bad, but anyone who had a tractor used that, and a couple of people rode down on horseback, and the search parties got organized really fast. One group ran down to launch the canoe and search the river, and other people made up teams to walk the banks. The ones with horses cantered off to look farther down. Irma opened the shop so people had somewhere dry to assemble. Someone called the police.

"You're soaked through," said Lovey, who'd come on her uncle's tractor. She got me some dry clothes from the storeroom out the back of the ambulance shed—don't ask me how she knew they were there, she just did. I couldn't stop shivering and Lovey took my hand for comfort, but she didn't have to say anything. We both knew how badly this could turn out. How badly the last time had gone. Everyone knew.

Then the two of us started to walk back to the river house, because I wanted to be with Mum; I knew she'd be worried sick when she found out, and people had already gone to the river house to see if Adrian had somehow got back. I didn't see how he could have; he didn't know the area at all. Even if he'd got out of the water he'd be lost as well as freezing cold, and it was going to be dark soon.

We'd got as far as the first clump of mangroves when I heard it—we both did. A loud slapping noise from the river, and then a kind of grunt. It was still raining so it was hard to see, but we stopped and stared hard toward the river.

"It could have been an oar?" suggested Lovey. "Maybe it's the canoe, out already, looking for him."

"They'd be calling out, though, wouldn't they?"

I listened again. I wondered if it could possibly be Adrian, stuck somehow, and trying to get our attention.

I can't be sure about what happened next, and neither can Lovey.

But I reckon we saw the taniwha.

If I had to swear to it, then I'd have to say I wasn't sure. But what I did see was—something.

A dark shape that lifted at the edge of the river. Something that started out looking like a curving ridge, or maybe like a fin. But when I blinked and looked again it had filled out that first space and grown into some kind of vast curving thing.

A whole stretch of the riverbank had just vanished or was blocked out. Or had changed into something else.

The dark shape grew bigger and expanded outward, and I realized it was immense. Bigger than anything I could imagine, with no limit and no ending.

And then it had gone. It's not like it disappeared back under the water. It just was there, and then it wasn't.

I shook myself and remembered where I was, and the first thing I noticed was Lovey's fingernails biting into the palm of my hand. She was shaking, like I was.

We looked at each other and didn't say anything. We did wait for a minute but nothing else happened, and when we got to the road a jeep passed us and someone shouted the news: They'd found Adrian in the river and the ambulance was taking him into the hospital.

"Not that he's hurt, April," said Rangimarie, who was sitting with Mum by the time we got into the house. "It's just to be sure, eh? He's freezing cold and maybe in shock as well. He needs checking out."

I hugged Mum and she hugged me back, but there was no time to say anything because she was off in the jeep to follow the ambulance to the hospital. And then I thought I could go, too, and see Nana, so I looked around for Dr. Gullick; I'd seen her car down at the corner. I found her by the side of the road trying to get reception on her cell phone. She said she'd take me and Lovey into the hospital, but, of course, Lovey couldn't go in to see Nana, and we'd both have to wait for her afterward, and was that all okay? Oh, and why didn't we both put on warm clothes before we went?

"You both look as pale and cold as if you'd seen a ghost," she scolded. "Honestly, you two, where's your common sense?" We meekly nodded and did what she said.

"This'll be my third change of clothes today," I said as we searched the bedroom drawers for sweaters. "Must be a record."

"It was, wasn't it?" said Lovey softly. She wasn't talking about clothes.

I nodded at her.

"You have to wonder . . ."

I finished her sentence for her.

"You have to wonder why? Yeah, me, too. If it was meant for us to see?"

"Well, you called it," said Lovey softly. "You called it, and it came."

I felt cold again.

She looked at me carefully.

"And my mum says your nana's got second sight. Maybe you've got it, too."

"You think I did this?" That was a scary thought.

Lovey wriggled into yet another one of Nana's sweaters, flipped her hair outside the collar, and grinned at me.

"Hey, maybe this sweater's got the power!" But then she got serious again.

"All I know is, no one else saw what we saw. You have to wonder, is all I'm saying."

We talked again at the hospital, waiting for me to go up and see Nana. I told Lovey what had happened with Adrian on the riverbank.

Lovey said, "Maybe the taniwha caught him, and then came to give him back again?"

I thought about that, and about how the taniwha had hung on to Hemi for company all those years ago, and I grinned at her.

"Well, who'd want Adrian, right? No fun having him around."

"Here's another idea," said Lovey lowering her voice. "You pushed him when he fell in the river, right? And he could have drowned, and then you'd have been sort of responsible? So maybe the taniwha gave him back *to you*."

I looked at her in horror.

"You can't be serious! That's a terrible thought!"

"Not necessarily," said Lovey straight-faced. "You don't have to keep him."

I started to giggle and so did Lovey, and we couldn't stop. We ended up sliding to the floor, helpless with laughter, until a nurse came to shush us. Then I went up and sat with Nana.

The nurses said she hadn't come around from the anesthetic, but when I took her hand gently she smiled without opening her eyes, and whispered, "Jessye girl." So she knew I was there. I held her hand, and watched her breathing, and listened to the machines hum and beep. She still smelled of hospitals instead of herself, and I felt like I'd walked into a parallel universe where nothing was right, and neither of us belonged.

The nurses said I should talk to her, so I did. I told her about the storm and about going out in it, and about trying to talk to the taniwha and how that had made me feel, and I told her that Joe had mended the washhouse door. And then I sang to her again, because I knew she'd like that if she could hear me.

We have a local version of the most famous Maori song ever written. It's really a love song, but it talks about crossing over a raging river to calm waters, so it was a good choice for the moment:

> *Pokarekare ana,*
> *nga wai a Hokianga,*
> *whiti atu koe hine—*
> *marino ana e.*

> *They're wild and choppy,*
> *the waters of the Hokianga,*
> *cross over them, girl—*
> *to where it's calm.*

When I got back downstairs, Mum was with Lovey in the waiting room. She jumped up and hugged me.

"We did the wrong thing, Jayjay," she sobbed into my neck. "It was wrong and bad and stupid and I want you to forget everything that I said, and everything Adrian said, and we'll just go back to square one, shall we?"

I hugged her back. I felt sorry for her; I didn't even blame her, but I didn't think I'd forget what had happened, either. I suddenly thought about explorers again, the ones who sailed off to discover new worlds. And now I thought I was like an explorer, after all—but what I was discovering was a new view of a familiar landscape. The landscape was me and Nana and Mum. I could suddenly see it clearly; better than I'd ever done before.

Mum said that Adrian seemed okay, although they were keeping him overnight for observation. "He's wrapped up in foil blankets!" she said brightly. "Like a marathon runner!"

Dr. Gullick drove us all back to Waimotu, and Lovey slept on the sofa again. Mum spent the night in Nana's bed; I knew she wouldn't mind.

First thing next morning, Mum phoned the hospital to check on Adrian. I heard her saying things like, "That can't be right!" and "Would you check again, please?" and "Well, put me through to the ward, then." When she finally got off the phone she walked straight outside without looking at us, and sat on the veranda, staring out at the river. After awhile I took her a cup of tea. I thought I knew what had happened.

She took the tea with a shaky smile. Her cheeks were wet but she wasn't crying anymore. She sipped in silence, and I sat down beside her and patted her shoulder.

"He's gone," Mum said bleakly. "He disappeared from

the hospital first thing this morning; he checked himself out. No message or anything, just the nurse said he was freaked out and had to get away from Waimotu—I don't know why."

"What did she mean?" It sounded odd.

Mum shrugged. "I don't know, I really don't. But we were having problems, anyway. You know, Jayjay, I'll be better off without him, I wouldn't be surprised." And she sort of squared her shoulders and smiled bravely at me, and had another sip of tea. I had to blink a bit to stop my own tears showing.

"Maybe he's just gone back to the house in Auckland? Maybe he'll be there when you get back?" I suggested, although I didn't really think so, and Mum didn't, either.

Poor Mum.

Mum got a ride down to the ferry landing—"I'm due back at work tomorrow, Jayjay, got to keep the wolf from the door!" She didn't ask me to go back with her, which was a relief. I'd have hated to turn her down when she was so sad, but no way could I leave Nana right now.

Lovey and I cleaned up the mess left from the dramas of the night before. Then we sat on the veranda with mugs of stew from the freezer, and looked out at the river. It was calm now, with only the faintest ripples running through it, and the pale sunlight caught every streak of light in it—from silver to gold to dark deep green. It looked like a river that had finally remembered its manners, and was behaving well.

"Hard to believe the difference from yesterday," I said.

Lovey nodded. "Hard to believe a lot of things," she added.

"You remember what you told me? That there was unfinished business between my family and the taniwha?"

Lovey nodded again.

"Well, then. Maybe this finishes it?"

"Like, Adrian was trying to get the land and the taniwha stopped him? And that's a fair return for taking Hemi?" Lovey suggested.

"Something like that." I grinned, remembering something Mum had said. "If it's true about Adrian being freaked out . . ."

Lovey laughed. "You probably freaked him out yourself, girl! Pushing him into the river like that! Scary, or what!"

But I thought it might have been the taniwha.

"Only one little corner of that whole picture's anywhere near the truth, girl," said Joe, when I told him what Mum and Adrian had said about the land. "And if you want my opinion, they're both nuts."

"Mum isn't nuts, Joe," I argued. I felt protective about her, like I always did. "She's just—she just gets swept into things, and then she can't tell what's right anymore."

He looked at me thoughtfully.

"And Adrian's not nuts, either," I added. "Mean as a snake and a bully and a liar. Not mad, though."

"Fair enough," Joe said, grinning. "A mean, lying

bully'll do fine for him now he's out of the hospital. You can't hit a man when he's down, of course, but now he's up again it's no holds barred."

He leaned back on the couch and glanced out the window, just like Nana did, and then turned back to me.

"Now—about Mina's land," he said. "I'll tell you enough to set your mind to rest, and then your nana can tell you whatever else she likes when she's back on her feet." And so he did.

Mum and Adrian had got it upside down, the way Joe explained it. Nana had put her land in a trust, like they'd discovered—but it wasn't really mine at all, and even if it had been I couldn't have done anything with it.

"That's the idea of the trust she chose," Joe said. "It's to protect the land and the person it's in trust for. Because Maori land's precious, and because you're too young to have legal control of it, Mina wanted to cover both those things, in case something happens to her before you've grown up. It isn't yours yet—you couldn't sell it or raise money on it, not at your age. Your mother couldn't whip control away from you, either; the trust would stop her. And the rest of what they said to you? Making you toe the line, getting a court to say what's what? Load of sheep dung. Like you say; the man's a liar and April—well, she's been misled. She deserves better, is all I'll say."

"So none of it's true?" I wanted to be sure.

"None of it's true," he repeated. "Oh, one day you might be worth something to someone, but right now . . ." He grinned at me and then made a thumbs-down gesture.

I pretend-punched him, and he cringed away from me in mock fear and said, "No! Not the river! Anything but that!"

I reckon lots of people will have a good story going now, about what happened that night. It's a small town; you can't keep secrets in it. So I guess I'll be teased about it for years, whatever I do. It could even turn into my new Maori name. Sometimes Maori names tell a bit of a story—like Toi-kai-rakau, for instance, which means Toi-the-wood-eater. I'll have to get Nana to help translate mine: Jessye-who-pushed-a-man-into-the-river.

Joe had a couple more things to say before he left.

"Don't forget to take the mail in to Mina next time you see her—it'll be before I can get over, I reckon." He gestured at the pile on the mantelpiece. "There's stuff here she'll want to know about."

He picked up his coat and shoved his hands in the pockets as he turned to the door. Then he paused and turned back again.

"Forgot this," he said, fumbling something out of his pocket in a closed fist. He looked at me for a moment, almost like he was waiting for something. Then he held out his hand, and opened his fingers.

A beautiful little hei-matau—a fishhook ornament, carved from bone—nestled in his palm like a jewel.

"Take it, girl."

I picked it up gently and held it up to the light. It was cool and creamy-smooth, carved with interlocking patterns, like a moko tattoo. I'd never seen anything as lovely. I turned to him with a question in my eyes, but I couldn't read his expression.

"It came out of the river with Adrian," Joe said evenly. "We dragged him out, down by the mangroves, and this came up, too. Caught on his hand."

He reached out and stroked it gently with one finger.

"Hemi's, I reckon. Had one just like it when he fell in. Show Mina when she's stronger; she'll recognize it." And then he nodded at me.

"It's yours now, girl," he said. "The taniwha's given it back, and from what I understand, it's yours now. Reckon you earned it."

Chapter Thirteen

Six days later I was sitting on the end of Nana's hospital bed. She was admiring the plastic-bag chicken, which I'd finished as well as I could and brought in to show her. I was enjoying the view from her window. You could see right across town to where the mountain started to rise from the flat coastal plain: our mountain, the one you cross to get back to Waimotu, which is where Nana was going in a few more days. Taking it slowly—but taking it, is what she said. She was a whole lot better.

I'd been catching her up bit by bit, every time I went in to see her. Telling her what had happened in stages; not wanting to upset her or slow down her recovery. I'd started with the big bit about Adrian and then back-tracked, and I jumped around and stopped until the next time if she looked tired. A bit like *The Arabian Nights,* but without the danger. That afternoon I was telling her about how I'd asked the taniwha for help.

Nana looked thoughtful. She pleated the sheet under her hands for a few moments, without saying anything. Then she said, "That was brave, Jessye girl."

I hadn't felt brave at the time; I'd just known I had to do it. But Nana saw it differently.

"All the fears and worries you carry around on your shoulders. Yourself and the world: a lot to be worried about, eh girl? Taking that out on a taniwha's quite something. But then, that's between you and the taniwha—private business, I reckon." She was teasing me a bit, but not much. I could see she thought it mattered.

"Do you think this one's real, then?"

Nana shifted around, finding a better spot on her pillows. Then she gave me a quick nod.

"I saw it, too, once. After Hemi drowned." She paused, and then shrugged the thought away, and brought up a hand to stop any questions I might ask.

"People say I've got second sight, should give me power, eh? It's not made me happy, I can tell you that—too much grief and loss through the years. So I don't wish it on you. Not that I can do anything about it one way or another. You've maybe got it; and if you do then you'll see more things in life than other people. Maybe more than you like. I can't stop that for you. But there's one thing I can put right for you, maybe, so I'm going to try."

I think I knew what she was going to say next. No second sight in it; nothing spooky at all—just ideas that had been sorting and shuffling around in my head and suddenly came together, like hands clasping. Or like a pattern in weaving.

"Mikey. Your dad. I've heard from him."

I didn't move.

"All that mail you brought me last week—there was a letter from him. Joe'll know; he'll have got one, too."

She sat up again so she could pat my hand.

"Jessye, this is a thing I've done wrong, even though I meant it for the best; meant to protect what he'd left behind." I knew she meant me. Suddenly there were tears in her eyes, and I leaned in to give her a hug.

"It's time to put it right," she repeated more firmly. "Now, Jessye girl, I have to tell you something else that's hard: Your dad's been in prison. He did something years ago; something I thought I couldn't forgive. But now I'm going to try, see if he'll let me. I've written back to him; told him about you; asked him to come and see us when he's released."

She sat back against her pillows and sighed for a moment with her eyes closed. She looked exhausted, but when she opened her eyes again she gave me a big smile.

"So let's hope he does, eh?"

"I don't see why you're not happy about this," Lovey said when I told her. She'd stayed on in Waimotu for the school holidays, because her mum had come down, too, with Moana. Lovey was still staying in the river house, though, and seeing her mum and sister every day. It was a good arrangement—I got to play with Moana and pretend I had a little sister, and Lovey and I got to play at being independent people with a house of our own.

"Why don't you just kick back, cuzzie, and see how it goes?" Lovey went on. "You might see your dad again, your nana's getting better, and you're living in Waimotu. What's not to like?" She tried for an American accent for the last bit and then broke out giggling.

I told her how confused I felt, even just about Dad—about him coming out of prison when I didn't even know that he'd gone in, let alone what for; what he'd done. Nana hadn't said, and I hadn't asked.

I could ask Joe, he might even tell me now because I've noticed he's changed a bit since the storm. He mentioned the taniwha to me like it was a real thing and not an old-fashioned story. Next thing, he'll be recycling.

But then again, I'm not sure I want to know why my dad's been in prison. It's the past, and I can't do anything about it. He's coming out and he has a life to put back together again. So I reckon I'll just wait while he does that.

I still felt gloomy, but Lovey wouldn't let me stay like that.

"Do what you can with what you have," she said. "People wanted to know if you were like your nana—now you know what they meant. You wanted to find out more about your dad—now you will, one way or another. You wanted your mum to break up with Adrian, stand more on her own two feet—it happened."

I looked at her carefully in case she was teasing me, sort of doing a *Hey! Your spooky powers are weirding me out.* But she wasn't.

"Don't spend your life wanting what you don't have," she said. Which is what Nana said to me, about Mum, years ago. And I remembered when Nana had said about making lemonade, which was saying the same thing in a different way. I also thought of another way to look at it.

My favorite Maori word is aroha. It means love, but it's a lot more than just the word. Aroha includes love of all kinds, between couples or between parents and children or brothers and sisters. It might be a whole family, or even the feeling in a group of people who aren't related; they just feel close. If one of them is in trouble the rest of the group come and help out. That's aroha.

You could say, it's like making lemonade: Everyone in your aroha are the ingredients, and you put them all together in your heart and make the best you can with them. Nana's my main ingredient, no question. And Lovey's in there, too, of course, and Joe, and Dr. Gullick. I could go on naming people who are part of my aroha. I guess my dad must be the secret ingredient.

I love Mum because she's my mum, and I couldn't not love her, even if I tried. And in a way I think I've let her down a bit because I didn't get her to see how wrong Adrian was for her; I lost my nerve over that one. But if I want her to let me do things my way now, I have to let her do things her way, too.

I'm going to stay on in the river house for now. I'm going to look after Nana and make sure she's a box of birds in no time, which is how she puts it. And there's another good thing on the horizon.

Lovey says her dad's going to be away a lot again next year as well as this one. He's got a big new court case com- ing up, and it'll probably go on even longer than the one he's on now. So Lovey and her mum and Moana *might* come and stay in Rangimarie's house up the road. And if it happens, Lovey's mum would have her own mum around to help with Moana, and Lovey and I *might* be able to go to the high school together on the bus. I'll go, anyway, but it would be great if Lovey came, too. We're good friends, Lovey and me. We support each other's differences—she makes me laugh more, and I make her think more. Like how the sweet-and-sour tastes work together in Nana's lemon cake, I reckon.

I'll always help Mum out if I can, no question, and I'll go and see her during the holidays, but I'll leave her be between times, and get on with my growing up. And maybe I'll be an artist—a weaver like Nana's mother or a painter like my mum, or maybe something else.

And I reckon one day soon my dad will come up the road from the ferry, and he'll walk into the river house and talk to Nana, and they'll start to put things right as far as they can.

And then? Well, I suppose we can go on from there, see if we can truly be part of one another's lives.

But in the meantime I'll wait and see what happens.

Nana's Lemonade

3 juicy lemons, washed and dried
1 lb (½ kilo) of sugar
5 teaspoons (25 grams) citric acid
6 cups (1½ litres) of water

If you have a food processor, peel the rind off of one of the lemons. You need to be careful to get only a thin layer of yellow rind—not the white pith underneath. Using a potato peeler helps. Then put the peel and a cup of sugar into the processor, and run it in bursts until the rind is ground up.

If you don't have a processor, grate the rind instead and mash it up with the sugar.

Put the rind and sugar mixture into a big saucepan. Squeeze all the lemons and mix the juice in as well. Then add the rest of the sugar, the citric acid, and the water. Heat the mixture, using an adult's help, and stir constantly until the sugar has dissolved. Then set it aside to cool, pour it into clean bottles, and store it in the fridge.

Use this like a cordial—one part of the lemonade mixture to three or four parts of water. Use sparkling mineral water or seltzer water if you want fizzy lemonade. You can add a bit more sugar if you like a sweeter drink. The lemonade in this recipe has a very lemony taste, even if the lemons you use aren't as juicy as the ones from Nana's tree.

Nana's Lemon Cake

For the cake:

the rind and 3–4 tablespoons of juice from 1 large lemon

¾ cup (200 grams) superfine (baker's) sugar

2 sticks (8 ounces) softened butter, plus a little more
to grease the loaf pan

1 cup (125 grams) plain flour

1 cup (125 grams) whole-wheat flour

2½ level teaspoons baking powder

¼ teaspoon salt

4 large eggs

For the syrup:

the rind and 2–3 tablespoons of juice from 1 lemon

⅔ cup (150 grams) superfine (baker's) sugar

First, heat the oven to 325°F and cover the bottom
and sides of an 8-inch loaf pan with a thin layer of
butter. Use a nonstick pan or line the buttered pan
with baking parchment.

Next, make the cake. If you have a food processor,
peel the lemon thinly with a vegetable peeler and
process the strips of rind with the sugar until the

peel turns into tiny yellow specks. If you don't have a processor, thinly grate the yellow part of the lemon rind into a large mixing bowl and stir in the sugar.

Chop the butter into small pieces and add them to the processor or the mixing bowl. Sift in the flours, the baking powder, and the salt. If you don't have a sifter, you can use a fine sieve. Then break in the eggs, one at a time, and finally pour in the lemon juice.

Process or beat the mixture until it is smooth, but don't process or beat it too long or the cake may be tough. Pour the mixture into the prepared loaf pan, smooth the top, and carefully put the pan into the center of the oven. Be sure to use the oven mitts, or ask an adult for help when inserting and removing the cake.

The cake will take about one hour to cook, but you should check on it after about 45 minutes. The cake is done when it has risen with a golden brown top and a fork stuck into the center of the cake comes out clean.

While the cake is cooking, get the syrup ready. Grate the rind and squeeze the second lemon. Put the rind and juice into the small mixing bowl with the sugar. Stir until the sugar starts to dissolve, and then set the bowl aside.

When the cake is done, remove the cake and turn it carefully out of the pan. Peel the baking parchment away if you used it, and then ease the cake gently into a shallow dish. Using a skewer or a fork, make little holes all over the top of the cake and spoon the syrup slowly over it. Don't worry if some syrup trickles into the dish. By the time the cake is cool it will have absorbed the syrup, leaving only a sugary topping.

Enjoy!

Glossary

aroha—love

haere mai—an informal greeting or farewell

haka—a fierce dance

hapu—a clan within an *iwi*, or tribe

hau—wind

hei-matau—an ornament carved in the shape of a fishhook

Hemi—the Maori translation of James

hui—a community meeting

hukanui—foaming water

ika—fish

iwi—tribe

kai—food

kaumatua—elders

karakia—a thanksgiving prayer

kia ora—an informal greeting

mahana—warm

manuka—a native New Zealand plant. Honey made from manuka flowers is dark and strongly flavored.

Maori—the indigenous people of New Zealand. Also, the language spoken by the Maori people.

marae—a traditional Maori community center, which is treated with great care and respect.

maroke—dry

Maui—a demigod from Maori mythology

mihimihi—a traditional formal Maori greeting

mokopuna—grandchild

Ngapuhi—a tribe of the Maori people

pahu—an alarm, such as a gong

ta moko—tattoo

tangi—a funeral

taniwha—a mythical marine creature such as a water monster

taonga—treasure

tena koe—a formal good-bye

tepu—table

Tu—Nana's cat, named after the Maori God of war

ua—rain

uira—lightning

wai—water

waiata—Maori songs

waiata tawhito—ancient chanted songs

waiwai—lots of water

waka—a canoe

whanau—a family group within a *hapu*, or clan

whatitiri—thunder